CHANCE FOR LOVE
A Gansett Island Novella

THE GANSETT ISLAND SERIES, BOOK 10.5

MARIE FORCE

Chance for Love
A Gansett Island Novella
The Gansett Island Series, Book 10.5
By: Marie Force

Published by HTJB, Inc.
Copyright 2014. HTJB, Inc.
Cover by Kristina Brinton
ISBN: 978-0991418213

All characters in this book are fiction and figments of the

author's imagination.

marieforce.com

AUTHOR'S NOTE

Were you wondering how I spent my Christmas vacation? Wonder no more! I was on Gansett Island with heartbroken billionaire Jared James. We got to know Jared in *Time for Love,* when David and Daisy befriended David's elusive landlord who'd come to the island seeking refuge after his girlfriend turned down his marriage proposal. We saw him again in *Meant for Love,* when he reconnected with Wharton classmate Jenny Wilks. Readers were eager to know more about the woman who'd broken Jared's heart, and they wanted to know what I had in store for him. The more I thought about his story, the more I realized what I needed to do. I hope you'll enjoy this brief visit with some Gansett Island friends as well as the introduction of a new couple.

I'm blessed to have the most amazing "Team Jack" in place, so when I finish a novella over Christmas vacation I can turn it around for readers two short weeks later. A million thanks go to Julie Cupp, CMP, who runs my business so incredibly well; Lisa Cafferty, CPA, my longtime friend and new CFO, who helps me sleep at night; Holly Sullivan, my dear friend and cohort in childrearing; Isabel Sullivan, my adorably wonderful niece, and her baby, Harper, who makes me smile like a loon every time I see her; Nikki Colquhoun, Julie's BFF, who has become my friend, too; and Cheryl Serra, my friend of more than twenty-five years, who is now handling public relations for me with her trademark good humor. I love you all, and I'm thrilled to be working with many of my favorite ladies every day.

Thanks also to my awesome Beta readers, who are so good to me: Ronlyn Howe, Kara Conrad, Anne Woodall and Holly Sullivan.

In addition to my personal team, I've gathered a group of wonderful, amazing contractors who drop everything for me every time I need them. Thanks go to cover designer *extraordinaire* Kristina Brinton; fabulous copy editor, Linda Ingmanson, who has been with me since the first of my nineteen self-published books; and Joyce Lamb, my new and truly outstanding proofreader. You ladies are the BEST, and I'm delighted to work with you.

Special thanks to my family, Dan, Emily and Jake, and my dad, George, who laughed at me for coming off a brutal deadline on December 20 and deciding to spend my "vacation" having "fun" writing a Gansett Island novella. Every minute I get to spend on Gansett is a joy for me, and I'm so very grateful to the readers who continue to come back for every new adventure I dream up. Much more to come from Gansett!

xoxo
Marie

CHAPTER 1

It's high time to end the pity party. That was the thought Jared James woke up with on the fortieth day after the love of his life turned down his marriage proposal.

On that Friday morning in late July, Jared woke to the sound of seagulls and surf pounding against the rocks that abutted his property on Gansett Island—and to this somewhat major development in the midst of his retreat from real life. As he did every morning, he thought of his girlfriend, Elisabeth—*"with an S,"* she always said. His ex-girlfriend now...

He'd called her Lizzie, a nickname she'd always hated until he decided she was *his* Lizzie. Over time, he'd convinced her she loved the nickname as much as she loved him. As he had every day since it all went so bad, he thought of the night he'd taken her to a rooftop restaurant in Manhattan, which had been reserved just for them. He recalled his carefully planned proposal and the look of utter shock and dismay on her face when she realized what he was asking.

She'd shaken her head, which meant *no* in every language he spoke. *She actually said no.* That was the part he still couldn't believe more than a month later. He hadn't seen that coming. It hadn't occurred to him for a second that she'd say no. When he'd gotten down on one knee, he'd pictured an entirely different outcome. He'd imagined a tearful acceptance, kissing and hugging and dancing.

There'd been champagne chilling for the celebration that hadn't happened. He'd had the company Learjet waiting at Teterboro to whisk her off to Paris for a romantic long weekend. She'd always wanted to go there, and he was set to make all her dreams come true, starting with that one.

She'd said *no*.

He hadn't heard much of what she said after she shook her head in reply to his heartfelt question. The movement of her head in a negative direction had hit him like a fist to the gut. There'd been tears, not the happy kind he'd hoped for, but rather the grief-stricken sort, the kind that come when everything that could go wrong did. He knew about those tears. He'd shed a lot of them over the last five weeks.

In all his thirty-eight years, he'd never shed a tear over a woman until he'd finally given his heart to one, only to see it crushed to smithereens after the best year of his life. He had vague memories of standing up, of staring at her tearstained face as she continued to shake her head and tried to make him understand.

But he hadn't heard a word she said. It was all noise that refused to permeate the fog that had infiltrated his brain. He'd walked away and taken a cab to the garage where he kept his car. He'd driven for hours to get the first ferry of the morning to the home he'd bought on Gansett Island a couple of years ago and had barely seen since. He'd been too busy to spend time on the island.

Now he had nothing but time after taking an indefinite leave of absence from work.

Lizzie had called him a couple of times since that night, but he hadn't taken her calls. What did it matter now? What could she possibly say that would make a difference? He'd erased her voice-mail messages without listening to them. The last thing he needed was to hear her voice and be set back to day one when he'd honestly wondered if he was going to be able to continue breathing without her.

Yeah, he was a mess, and he was sick to death of being a mess. He was sick to death of himself. He got up and pulled on shorts and a tank, shoved his feet into an old pair of Nikes and headed out to run on the beach, something he'd done nearly every day he'd been here. What the hell good was owning waterfront property if you didn't take advantage of the chance to run on the beach?

He hadn't taken the time to appreciate most of the perks of making a billion dollars before his thirty-fifth birthday. He'd been too busy making more money to enjoy what he'd already accomplished. Those days were over, too. In the weeks he'd spent on Gansett, he'd been able to *breathe* for the first time in longer than he could remember. Without the constant pressure of work, work and more work, he'd discovered he had absolutely no life away from work.

He didn't have a single hobby, and he didn't have many friends who weren't affiliated in some way with his job. His clients were among his closest friends. How screwed up was that? Lizzie had been the exception. He'd met her at a benefit for the homeless shelter she ran for women and children in crisis. One of the guys from work had talked him into sponsoring the event, which was how he'd ended up in a monkey suit on a Wednesday evening, working the ballroom in the Ritz-Carlton at Central Park.

If he lived forever, Jared would never forget the first time he saw her. He'd been talking with some friends, guys he knew from the financial rat race, while his gaze swept the room and landed on her. She'd worn black—slinky, sexy black—that showed off her subtle curves.

However, her curves, as captivating as they'd been, hadn't been the thing that made him walk away from a conversation mid-sentence. No, it had been her smile and the way it lit up her entire face that had him making his way across the crowded room, like a magnet drawn to the most precious of metals.

"Why am I thinking about that?" he asked himself as he pounded his footprints into the sand. "I'm done thinking about her, reliving every minute I spent with her. It's over, and it's time to accept that and stop acting like a pussy-whipped, pathetic, ridiculous fool. She doesn't want you. Plenty of others do."

Except… He didn't want anyone else. He'd never wanted anyone the way he wanted her, and it was going to take a lot more than forty days for the yearning to subside. Still, that didn't mean he had to walk around like a lovesick dickwad in the meantime.

He barely noticed the gorgeous scenery that unfolded before him as he hit the mile mark and turned back, a plan forming as he went. He'd invite some people over for dinner. They'd have a cookout like normal people did this time of year. David and Daisy would come, and he'd ask Jenny Wilks and her fiancé, Alex Martinez. He'd tell them to bring others who'd like a free steak and a couple of beers.

People, he thought. That's what he needed. David and Daisy had been exceptionally good friends to him, dragging him along on many a date night and letting him be their official third wheel. The least he could do was make them dinner to thank them for their extraordinary compassion as he nursed his broken heart.

He came to a halt at the stairs that led to his house, bent at the waist to catch his breath and then walked slowly up the stairs and across the lawn, past the inground pool he'd never used. A guy came out from the mainland every week to tend to it. Perhaps it was time someone actually swam in the crystal-clear water he paid a small fortune to maintain.

Grasping the hem of his tank, he brought it up to wipe the sweat off his face. When he let the shirt drop, he noticed David coming down the stairs from the garage apartment.

"Off to save some lives, Doc?" Jared asked his friend, who was dressed in khakis and a blue dress shirt—or what Daisy called his doctor uniform.

"You know it," David said, his face lifting into the engaging grin that had become familiar to Jared in the last few weeks.

"Hey, so why don't you and Daisy come for a cookout tonight? You can take a swim and have a steak. If you want to."

David eyed him skeptically. "Who's cooking?"

"I am," Jared said indignantly. "I'm not totally useless."

Laughing, David said, "No comment. Daisy will want to know what we can bring."

"You don't have to bring anything."

"That won't fly with her. How about a salad?"

"Sure." Jared had come to know Daisy well in the last few weeks and recognized defeat when he saw it. "Sounds good."

"Great. What time?"

"Six thirty?" That sounded like a good time for a cookout, didn't it?

"We'll be here."

"If there's anyone else you want to bring, feel free."

"Maybe I'll ask Victoria at the clinic. She's fun."

"Not a fix-up, right?"

David tossed his head back and laughed. "Hardly. She's hot and heavy with an Irishman."

"Tell her to bring him."

"I'll do that." David gave him a perusing look. "You seem better."

"I think it's more that I'm sick of feeling like shit. That gets old after a while."

"Yes, it does."

David had shared what he'd gone through after he'd screwed up his relationship with his fiancée and then had to sit on the sidelines and watch while she married someone else.

"Does it ever stop hurting like hell?" Jared asked.

"Eventually."

Hands on his hips, Jared nodded. "Good to know. See you tonight?"

"We'll be there. Thanks for the invite."

"Thanks for everything. You and Daisy have been… You've been great. Really great."

"I'm glad to finally get to know the guy I've been sending my rent checks to all this time," David said with a smile as he headed for his car with a wave from Jared.

Clinging to the upbeat attitude he'd woken with, Jared went to the outdoor shower to rinse off the sweat and sand. He'd owned the house for three years but hadn't discovered the outdoor shower until he'd arrived earlier in the summer.

"I need to remember how to enjoy life," he muttered as he stood under the cool water and looked up at the bright sunshine. Other than the incredible time he'd spent with Lizzie, he'd given everything he had to his work for so long he'd forgotten the simple pleasure of an early morning run on the beach. It was quite possible that he'd never get over losing Lizzie, but there was no sense in letting what remained of his life be ruined by her rejection.

He'd recently reconnected with Jenny Wilks, a woman he'd known at UPenn's Wharton School where he'd studied for his MBA. Jenny had lost her fiancé, Toby, who Jared had also known at Penn, in the 9/11 attacks on New York City. The reminder of Toby's untimely death made Jared feel guilty for spending glorious summer days grieving for a woman who clearly didn't love him as much as he'd loved her.

Jared sat on a lounge chair by the pool and let the warm sun dry him as he plotted his day. First stop, grocery store. Second stop, liquor store. When was the last time he'd been anywhere near a grocery or liquor store? He couldn't recall. In the city, he had a household staff who took care of such things for him. Here on the island, his cleaning lady started bringing groceries with her when she realized he wasn't eating much of anything as he nursed his broken heart.

"Enough with being a pathetic loser." He got up to go get dressed and head out on his errands. He had a party to get ready for.

On the way into town, Jared's attention was drawn to an Open House sign outside the Chesterfield Estate, which he'd read about in the *Gansett Gazette*. The twenty-acre parcel had been for sale for quite some time, and he had to admit he was curious, especially after hearing Alex and Jenny talk about it.

Since he had all day before his guests were due to arrive, he decided to indulge the curiosity and pulled down the long driveway that led to the enormous stone house on the Atlantic coast.

Jared had seen some incredible houses in his time, had been a guest at some of the most exceptional seaside homes in the Hamptons, but he'd never seen anything quite like this one. A blonde woman dressed in a sharp black suit worked the door. Jared noticed she took a quick look at him, dressed in faded cargo shorts and an old polo shirt, and dismissed him on first glance.

Part of him wanted to tell her he could buy the estate a thousand times over if he so desired, but he resisted the urge to brag and took the brochure that she handed to him.

"Make yourself at home," she said with a tight, disinterested smile.

"Thank you." Jared had the house to himself as he wandered through spacious, airy rooms. In the brochure, he noted that Harold Chesterfield, an oilman, had built the summer house in 1932 as a surprise for his bride, Esther, who had died a couple of years ago. A black-and-white photo of the happy couple tugged at Jared's broken heart.

When he thought about all the things he could've given his beloved Lizzie… Except she'd never wanted such things from him. Her discomfort with his affluence and fondness for the finer things in life had been the only source of discontent in what had been an otherwise blissful relationship. He'd wanted to give her everything, to shower her in diamonds and whisk her away to places she'd only dreamed of visiting.

Over and over again, however, she'd told him she didn't want those things. She wanted him but had no interest in his extravagant lifestyle. The one comment that had permeated the fog after the proposal-gone-wrong had haunted him ever since: *"I can't live like you do. I just can't."*

"Why are you thinking about her again?" Jared muttered to himself. He'd be a raving lunatic by the time he finally emerged from his self-imposed exile. That was what she'd reduced him to.

As he walked through one incredible room after another, an idea occurred to him and solidified when he reached the grand staircase in the center of the magnificent house.

"Are you finding everything all right?" the frosty blonde asked when she found him in the drawing room, staring at the brochure like he gave a damn about the Chesterfields and their "storybook" romance.

"What's the asking price?" It was the one thing he couldn't find anywhere in the literature.

"It's listed at fifteen nine."

Jared wondered how Jenny and Alex would feel about getting married here. They'd lamented that nothing was available on short notice for a wedding this summer. Ironic, right, to be thinking about another couple's wedding when he'd expected to be planning his own. *You're not thinking about that...*

"Would they take fourteen five?"

The blonde's mouth fell open in shock and then closed just as quickly when she recovered her composure. "And you are?"

"Jared James."

"Oh! Mr. James! I didn't recognize you! I'm so sorry. I'm Doro Chase, representing the Chesterfields' heirs."

Jared shook her hand but only because she'd thrust it practically into his chest in her excitement.

"I can't believe I didn't recognize you!"

"Anyway, about the offer... Are your clients willing to negotiate?"

"I'm sure they'd be willing to entertain your offer. I'd be happy to discuss it with them if you're serious."

Jared took in the view of the ocean, the sweeping stairway, the incredible woodwork, the huge rooms, the hardwood floors. The place called to the businessman in him and filled him with the kind of enthusiasm he hadn't felt in weeks. "I'm serious."

CHAPTER 2

This is a fool's errand, Elisabeth Sutter decided as the wind whipped through her hair as she stood at the bow of the ferry and watched Gansett Island come into view. After all, nothing had changed since she'd last seen Jared. He was still richer than God, and she still had no desire to be married to that kind of money.

Sure, money made everything easier, but sometimes it made things *too* easy and far too crazy for her liking. If only she could've forgotten about him, the real him, the man behind the money, the man she'd fallen desperately in love with and then tried to let go of because it had seemed like the right thing to do.

How wrong she'd been. She'd known almost immediately that she'd made a terrible mistake. The look on his face when he realized she was declining his beautiful proposal… That look was now seared permanently into her memory bank, along with the pain he'd worn in the incredibly expressive eyes that had always gazed at her with unabashed love.

That she could've done that to him… It still made her sick to think about the pain she'd caused him, the pain she'd caused them both. If only she hadn't been so hasty to reject him. If only she'd taken a minute to process her thoughts before reacting so negatively. If only, if only.

It had taken nearly six weeks of daily visits to his office before his personal assistant had finally buckled and told her where he was.

Elisabeth hadn't even known about the house on Gansett Island, which more or less proved her point about why their relationship would never work long term. Sometimes she felt as though there was more about him she *didn't* know than what she did know. And what she knew of him, she loved. That was the simple truth she'd lived with since the last time she saw him.

She loved him. After the last disastrous evening they'd spent together, she'd tried to talk herself out of loving him. Not loving him was easier, cleaner, simpler. Their lifestyles were as diametrically different as two lives could be. She was low-budget, low-key, low-maintenance. He was all cash, dash and flash.

And she loved him.

Elisabeth blew out a deep breath that was swallowed by the breeze whipping her hair into knots as the ferry closed the distance between the mainland and Gansett. By now, he probably hated her and had forgotten all the reasons why he'd once wanted to marry her.

That was why she thought of this as a fool's errand. What good could possibly come of showing up out of the blue forty days after she'd rejected him so profoundly? What was she thinking coming here? What did she hope to achieve? None of the things that truly mattered had changed. He still had more money than God, and she was still unwilling to change who she was to suit his billionaire lifestyle.

She ran a homeless shelter, for crying out loud. How did that jibe with the life of a Wall Street tycoon who made money as effortlessly as most people breathed? From the very start she'd found their divergent paths in life to be comical—and worrisome. They'd joked about their differences as they'd gotten to know each other. But the longer they were together, the more glaring the differences had become.

He hadn't cared about any of that. He'd told her he'd give her anything and everything she wanted if only she'd marry him and vow to love him forever. She'd begun shaking her head before he'd even finished his proposal.

Elisabeth's eyes burned with tears that couldn't be blamed on the wind. She feared that negative head shake would turn out to be the single greatest mistake she'd ever make in her life. Somehow, some way, she had to tell him that. He needed to know that she regretted it. She wasn't sure she was willing to change her answer, but she couldn't let him think she didn't love him.

That was why she'd taken four trains every day for weeks to get to his office. His assistant, Marcy, always knew where he was. He'd told her that the first week they met. If ever she couldn't get in touch with him, call Marcy, he'd said. Marcy had standing orders to put through Elisabeth's calls no matter what she might be interrupting.

Elisabeth had felt honored that he wanted to hear from her so badly that he didn't care if she interrupted his work. Marcy had been far less accommodating after the "disaster," as Elisabeth thought of that night on the rooftop when she'd ruined everything with the shake of her head.

Marcy had made her work for it, finally relenting when Elisabeth begged her to tell her where Jared was so she could attempt to fix the awful mess she'd made of things. "If you hurt him again," Marcy had said as she handed over the slip of paper that contained the one thing Elisabeth needed more than anything, "I'll find you, and I'll kill you."

"I understand," Elisabeth had said, knowing she deserved nothing less than death threats from Jared's faithful employee and friend.

"I don't think you do," Marcy had said. "But when you go there and you see him, you'll get it, and you'll know I mean it."

Marcy's statement indicated the breakup had been as bad for him as it'd been for her—probably worse, in fact, because he didn't know she still loved him as much as she ever had. He didn't know that she regretted her actions that night more than she'd ever regretted anything. He didn't know that she'd give everything she had—which wasn't much—to go back in time to rewrite the outcome of that night.

Watching the ferry dock in the picturesque port of Gansett, Elisabeth felt like she was going to be sick. The sun had dipped toward the horizon during her passage, casting a warm orangey glow over the town as people followed the cars and bikes off the boat.

"This is it," she whispered to herself as she stepped foot onto Gansett Island for the first time. She knew a moment of complete paralysis as she tried to figure out her next move. And then she shook it off and made her way to the taxi line, where a friendly looking older man with a shock of white hair and bright blue eyes waved her over to his woody station wagon.

"Give ya a lift?" he asked. His eyes lit up with mirth when he smiled, and his friendliness provided some badly needed comfort.

"Yes, please." Elisabeth handed him the slip of paper on which Marcy had written Jared's island address.

The cabbie let out a low whistle. "Nice place." With a courtly bow, he opened the back door for her and held it until she was settled.

Elisabeth wasn't surprised to hear that Jared's place was nice. Of course it was. It was probably the nicest house on the entire island. He wouldn't settle for anything less than the best. That was one of his personal mottos—and one she'd often taken issue with as she taught him the fine art of bargain living in the city.

"Where ya here from?" the kindly driver asked in a charming New England accent.

"New York City."

"Long way from home. Not much of nothin' here compared ta there."

How could she tell him that everything that mattered to her was here? "It's very pretty."

"That it tis. What brings ya ta our little island?"

"I'm coming to see a friend, and I'm hoping he'll be glad to see me." Now she was sharing her personal business with a perfect stranger, proof she'd gone totally around the bend.

"He'd be a fool ta not be happy ta see a pretty gal like yerself."

Elisabeth smiled for the first time in longer than she could remember and caught his wink in the rearview mirror. "He's not too happy with me at the moment, so he may not be glad to see me." There was something about the older man, something sweet and compassionate, that had her telling him the whole sordid tale.

"Well, now," he said, "I can see why ya think he might not be happy ta see ya after all that."

His words deflated the tiny bit of optimism she'd carried with her on this fool's errand.

"However, it's quite possible he'll be thrilled ta see ya, 'specially if yer here ta make things right with him."

"I want to make things right, if I can. I just hope it's not too late."

"If he loves ya, really, *really* loves ya, it's never too late."

Just like that she was once again filled with optimism, because the one thing she was absolutely sure of was that before she'd screwed it all up, Jared James had really, *really* loved her.

The driver used his blinker to signal a right turn into a long driveway. "Here ya are, honey." Jared's prized Porsche and several other cars were parked in front of the garage, so the cab driver stopped behind them and put his car in park. He turned to face her and handed her a business card. "If things don't work out the way ya want them ta, ya call me, and I'll come back fer ya."

Touched by his sweetness, Elisabeth glanced at the card. "Thank you, Ned. I'm Elisabeth, and I really appreciate you listening to my blathering."

"Not at'all, Lisbeth. I got two girls of my own. I understand the need ta talk it out."

"I guess you do." Elisabeth eyed Jared's big, beautiful contemporary home with trepidation. "Now that I'm here, I'm sort of scared of what might happen."

"If ya don't go in, ya'll never know."

"Here goes nothing," Elisabeth said as she reached for the door handle. "Oh my goodness, I'm about to get out and I haven't paid you!"

"Go on, doll. 'Twas my pleasure to bring ya here."

"I wouldn't feel right."

"Ya'll hurt my feelins if ya try to pay me."

"Well, if you put it that way..."

"I insist."

"Thank you so much—for the ride and the ear." Elisabeth got out of the car, toting her purse and the backpack she'd brought on the outside chance that he didn't turn her away. She'd have to find somewhere to stay if he did. The last ferry left in an hour.

While she stared at the house, Ned received a call for a ride from the dispatcher. "I'm a phone call away if ya need anything while yer here."

"Thanks again."

He backed out of the driveway and left with a wave as Elisabeth stood there stupidly trying to muster the courage to see this mission through to the bitter end.

She followed music to the back of the house, where she encountered a party in progress. Actually, calling it a party would be generous. Jared was entertaining two blonde women in bikinis in the pool. They were playing an animated game of volleyball with an oversize beach ball. He was laughing at something one of them said.

As she stood frozen in place, he picked up one of the women by the waist and tossed her into the deep end. She came up sputtering and swam after him, clearly seeking revenge as he howled with laughter and tried to dodge her efforts to catch him.

Elisabeth couldn't look away from his handsome, smiling face as he dove away from the woman who sought revenge.

Clearly, he was getting along just fine without her. She forced herself to look away, to stop staring at him like the lovesick idiot she had no right to be. She'd come here looking for closure, and she'd gotten it. He'd moved on. That was good. The thought of him heartbroken and decimated by her rejection was not the image of him she wanted to carry with her into the lonely future that stretched out before her.

Tears rolled down her face as she turned and walked back to the main road, clutching Ned's card in her hand. Fumbling with her cell phone, she placed the call. Thankfully, he didn't ask any questions and told her to wait for him by the mailbox, that he'd be back as soon as he could get there.

He didn't express sympathy or anything else that would take her over the edge she was clinging to with her fingertips. Tears slipped from her eyes, and she brushed them away angrily. What right did she have to cry over him frolicking in a pool with two gorgeous blondes? She'd made her own bed. Now she'd have to lie in it alone.

CHAPTER 3

"I don't feel right leaving Hope to deal with Mom tonight," Alex Martinez said as David drove him to meet his fiancée at Jared's house.

David had gone to the Martinez home to check on Alex's mother, Marion, who suffered from dementia. She'd had a particularly rough day, and Alex had asked him to come by on his way home to make sure there was no medical reason for her increased confusion.

"Hope is great with her," David said. "And you hired her so you could get some relief."

"I know, but I still don't feel right about leaving Hope to manage Mom after the day she's already had."

"You and Paul are still getting used to the fact that you now have help, so it's only natural you'd feel like there's something you're supposed to be doing for your mom. However, tonight you've got plans with your fiancée and your friends. That's what you need to be doing. It's okay to give yourself permission to have some fun, Alex."

"I guess so." Alex scratched wearily at the stubble on his jaw. "No matter what I'm doing, I feel guilty about what I *should* be doing. Mom doesn't even know I'm there most of the time, but I feel like I should be with her rather than at a cookout."

"Let me ask you this… In her right mind, what would your mom say to a statement like that?"

"She'd tell me I'm being ridiculous," Alex said with a grunt of laughter.

"There you go." David had known Marion Martinez—and her sons—all his life, and he had no doubt that Mrs. Martinez would hate to see her sons putting their lives on hold to take care of her. They'd ensured she was well cared for by hiring Hope Russell, a nurse from the mainland, to live onsite to help out with their mother's care. They continued to oversee all aspects of her medical situation, even with Hope now onboard. "She'd want you both to be happy."

"I hate this."

"I know. I hate it for you."

"What did she ever do to deserve such an awful affliction?" Alex asked with a sigh.

"Absolutely nothing. That's the bitch of it." David took a series of turns that led to Jared's waterfront estate, where he'd been lucky to score the garage apartment. He loved the place and had enjoyed getting to know Jared this summer. "Is Paul coming tonight?"

"He said he'd try. He's got some meeting with the land trust or something."

"He's Mr. Gansett Island, huh?" David said with a chuckle.

"That he is. I don't know how he does it all—runs the business, helps take care of Mom and volunteers so much time to the town council and all the accompanying demands. Those council meetings would bore me to tears, but he loves it all."

"The town needs people like him to protect what we've got here. I'm glad he's on the job."

Alex nodded in agreement. "He's dedicated. That's for sure."

"How're the wedding plans coming along?" Alex and his fiancée, Jenny, were hoping to be married in the next couple of months.

"Not so good. Everything is booked years in advance on this island."

"Why can't you do it at the lighthouse?" David asked. Until her recent move to live with Alex and his family, Jenny had been the lighthouse keeper at the Southeast Light. Now she was managing the retail portion of Martinez Lawn & Garden while she and Alex made plans to build a house next to his childhood home.

"The town is skittish about the liability of having a wedding out there. Something about drinking and nearby cliffs."

David laughed at the disgust he heard in Alex's voice.

"As if we wouldn't take steps to ensure none of our drunken guests pitched off the cliffs."

"I've had the unhappy luck of tending to a number of people who've pitched off our unforgiving cliffs," David said. "I hate to say the town might have a point…"

"You would side with them," Alex joked. "Mac and Maddie offered up their yard, but Jenny doesn't love that idea. It's a lot to ask of them."

"I'm sure you'll figure something out," David said as he slowed to take the turn into the driveway that led to Jared's estate. A woman standing by the mailbox had him stopping the car. Something about her was familiar. She was tall and slender with silky brown hair that fell just past her shoulders. As he opened the window, he noticed she was crying. "Hi there. Can I help you with something?"

"Oh no," she said, wiping the tears from her face. "I'm waiting for a cab."

"Have we met?"

"No, I don't think so."

"You look really familiar to me." And then he remembered where he'd seen her… in pictures Jared had shared with him and Daisy. She was Jared's Lizzie, and she was standing at the end of his driveway waiting for a cab. David put the car in park and got out. "I'm David Lawrence, a friend of Jared's. You're his Lizzie, right?"

She gasped and shook her head. "I'm not his anything. I'm Elisabeth."

"Have you been to see him?" David asked gently, careful to avoid saying something that would upset her even more.

"Not exactly. He's very busy entertaining a couple of beautiful, busty blondes in bikinis."

The bitterness in her tone took him by surprise. Busty blondes? Jared had been too busy nursing his shattered heart to entertain anyone until today. Suddenly, he realized who she must be referring to and was forced to hold back a laugh. "Um, I think you might be referring to my girlfriend and his fiancée," David said, using his thumb to point at Alex, who'd waited in the car.

To his credit, Alex waved and smiled.

"Y-your girlfriend?" she asked, her voice wavering as new tears filled her eyes.

"Yes, my girlfriend, Daisy, and his fiancée, Jenny. We're meeting them here. Alex and I were detained, so we sent them on ahead to give Jared a hand getting ready for the cookout he suddenly decided to have today after weeks of moping around."

"H-he's been moping?"

"He's been heartbroken." David hoped he was doing the right thing by telling her the truth about what a mess Jared had been. "I know for a fact he'd absolutely love to see you."

"He would? Really?"

"Really. Could I give you a lift to the house?"

She seemed frozen with indecision as she contemplated his offer. "I have a cab coming to take me back to town."

"You could cancel that. If you decide you want to go to town later, I'll take you myself. No questions asked."

"Oh, you will?"

"Standing offer, but knowing how sad Jared has been without you, I doubt you'll need to take me up on it."

"He's sad, not angry?"

"He's very sad. I haven't seen any anger. Doesn't mean it isn't there, but all I've seen is the sadness."

"I hate that I did that to him," she said softly.

"You should tell him that. I think it would matter to him."

Nodding, she retrieved her cell phone and put through the call to cancel her cab.

David relieved her of her backpack and held the back door to his car for her. When she was settled, he handed her the backpack.

"Thank you."

"No problem." David got in the car and sneaked a wide-eyed look at Alex, who'd watched the entire scene unfold. At the end of the driveway, he parked in his spot next to Jared's sharp-looking black Porsche. Jenny's car was also in the driveway, behind Jared's. The three of them got out and followed the sound of voices, laughter and music to the pool area, where Jared was indeed in the midst of a spirited game of beach volleyball with Jenny and Daisy.

None of them noticed the new arrivals until they walked through the gate to the fenced-in pool deck.

"Hey!" Jared said. "You made it. Don't you own a bathing suit, Doctor David?"

"In fact I do, but I found a friend of yours on the way in."

Jared's gaze shifted from David to Lizzie, who stood between him and Alex. Along with the shock that registered on Jared's face, David also saw love and longing and knew he'd done the right thing by persuading her to come talk to Jared.

"Lizzie…" Jared said when he'd recovered the ability to speak.

"Hello, Jared."

Overcome by the sight of her, Jared lifted himself out of the pool and reached for a towel he'd tossed onto a chair earlier. "What're you doing here?" On first glance, he could see that she was thin, painfully thin, and he was immediately concerned. She'd confessed to a teenage eating disorder, and the thought of her battling that again—maybe because of him—struck a note of fear in his heart.

"I came to see you."

"Why?"

Lizzie took an uncertain look around at the four curious faces watching them. "I need to talk to you."

"We should go and let you guys talk," Jenny said as she took the hand Alex offered to help her out of the pool.

"No," Jared said, never taking his eyes off Lizzie. "We have plans. I got steak. We're having our cookout."

"Jared," David said. "It's fine. We can do it another night."

Weeks of pain and frustration and more than a little bit of anger boiled to the surface all at once as he stared at the face that had haunted him during forty sleepless nights. *"No,"* he said more emphatically this time. "We're having dinner."

"I'm sorry," Lizzie said, taking a step back. "I've come at a bad time. I'll just go…"

"You don't have to go," Jared said more softly. "It would be nice if you joined us."

"Oh, um, I don't want to intrude."

"You're not," he assured her, terrified at the thought of her leaving before he could hear what she'd come to say. "You've met David Lawrence and Alex Martinez. This is David's girlfriend, Daisy Babson, and Alex's fiancée, Jenny Wilks. Ladies, this is Elisabeth Sutter. Lizzie."

Jenny's mouth curved into a stunned O.

"So nice to meet you," Daisy said as she shook Lizzie's hand.

Jared was hardly surprised that the always-compassionate Daisy automatically welcomed Lizzie, despite the fact that she knew the whole ugly story. Jenny was also friendly and welcoming, if a bit more reserved about it than Daisy had been.

The girls donned beach cover-ups while Jared knotted the towel around his waist. "Let's get some drinks," he said as he led the way to the deck where he'd chilled a couple of twelve-packs of beer along with some white wine. "What can I get everyone?"

The guys helped themselves to beers while Jenny expertly uncorked a bottle of chardonnay that she shared with Daisy. "Lizzie?" she asked, holding up the bottle.

"She prefers the pinot grigio," Jared said. "I'll get it." His heart beat fast and erratically as he tried to resist the need to stare at her, to drink in the familiar sight of her. He walked inside on shaky legs, his entire body tingling from the shock, the excitement, the need to know… What was she doing here? And why had she been crying?

David followed him inside. "Are you okay?"

"I… I don't know what I am. Did she say anything about why she's here?"

"Isn't that rather obvious?"

Jared poured himself a shot of top-shelf whisky and downed it before pouring another one. "No. It's not." The heat of the liquor traveled through his system, calming his nerves.

"Alex and I found her out by the road. She'd been here, saw you in the pool with Daisy and Jenny, jumped to a bunch of incorrect conclusions and had called for a cab to take her back to town. I recognized her from the photos you showed me."

When Jared realized how close he'd come to never knowing she'd been there at all… And then he remembered the rare moments of frivolity and laughter in the pool. It must've looked pretty bad to her, especially in light of his past reputation as a bit of a playboy. That life had ended the moment he'd laid eyes on her, and she knew it. Or she'd *known* it when they were together. He'd made sure of it.

"She was crying," David said. "She'd seen you with other women, and it upset her."

"You told her—"

"We set her straight. My girlfriend. His fiancée. We talked her into coming back with us."

"Thank you for that." Jared let his gaze wander through the kitchen-sink window to the deck where Jenny, Alex and Daisy had included Lizzie in their conversation. She looked slightly less uncomfortable than she had a few minutes ago.

"We should take off, Jared. You guys have stuff to talk about."

"It'll keep until later. I promised you dinner."

"Jared…"

"I need a little time to get my head together before I talk to her. It would help if you stayed."

"If you're sure…"

"I'm sure."

"By the way, I might've let it slip that you've been a bit of a mess since you got here. I hope that's okay."

"She may as well know the truth."

"Whatever happens, I hope you get what you want."

Looking at her sitting on his deck, surrounded by his friends, Jared was no longer certain of what he wanted from her. She'd hurt him badly. He wasn't sure if he could risk letting her back in—if that was why she'd come—only to have it happen again. "Thanks, man. You and Daisy have been so great. I don't know what I would've done without you."

"It's been fun for us, too. Now, you'd better get out there with her wine or she might think you aren't happy to see her. You are happy to see her, aren't you?"

Happy might not be the right word. Confused, agitated, uncertain... But happy? First he needed to know why she'd come. Then he'd decide how he felt about it. "Yeah," he said simply. That was all he had at the moment. He uncorked the bottle of pinot and followed David back to the porch with an extra glass in hand.

Victoria and her charming Irishman joined them a short time later, as did Alex's brother, Paul, who brought funny stories from his meeting with an elderly island resident who'd talked for two straight hours, without pause, in support of a parcel the land trust had no plans to develop. Jared had offered him a glass of whisky, which he'd accepted gratefully.

They ate the steak, baked potatoes and salad, swam in the pool, sat by the fire and toasted marshmallows. His friends teased him about how he'd bought every kind of salad dressing offered in the grocery store and how he'd have to eat salad for a year to use them all. Jared took their teasing in stride while he tried to relax and enjoy the gathering, but a humming awareness of Lizzie had him preoccupied as he watched her stare into the fire. She'd participated in the conversation, laughed at Shannon O'Grady's hilarious quips, eaten a few bites of dinner and had a second glass of wine.

But Jared knew her well enough to sense she was as on edge as he was, anticipating—and probably dreading—what would happen after his friends left.

David stood at ten thirty, extended his hand to Daisy and helped her up. "I gotta work in the morning," he said regretfully. "I need my beauty sleep." He turned to Lizzie. "It was really nice to meet you."

"You, too. Thanks for... Well, thanks."

"My pleasure."

Daisy, being Daisy, took it a step further and hugged Lizzie, who seemed surprised but pleased by the gesture. Then Daisy hugged Jared and whispered in his ear, "Good luck."

"Thanks." She was so sweet and so caring and had been a very good friend to him in the last few weeks. At her insistence, Jared had become the "other man" in her relationship with David. She'd forced him out of his cocoon and dragged him along on many a date, which he'd appreciated more than she could ever know.

"We should go, too," Alex said. "I've got to work in the morning. No rest for the landscapers this time of year."

Paul groaned in agreement.

"Before you go," Jared said to Alex and Jenny, "I think I might've found a place for you to have your wedding."

Jenny perked right up and lifted her head off Alex's shoulder. "Speak to me."

"Have you thought about the Chesterfield place?"

Jenny's smile dimmed. "That was our first choice, but we were shot down because it's on the market. It's not available for events."

"I heard it might be getting a new owner and that he'd be amenable to a wedding there."

Jenny stared at him, agape. "Did you *buy* the Chesterfield Estate?"

"I might've made an offer."

"*Why?*"

"Because you need a place to get married, and it seemed perfect. Have you seen the gardens?"

Jenny and Alex exchanged a glance along with small, private smiles. "We have," she said. "My fiancé takes exquisite care of them."

"He does a brilliant job," Jared agreed.

"So, let me get this straight," Alex said. "We needed a place for our wedding, so you *bought* the Chesterfield Estate?"

"I made an offer," Jared said, trying not to squirm as they all stared at him, no one more intently than Lizzie. "It'd be a great place for a wedding, but it's also a hell of an investment. The place is incredible."

Jenny sniffled and dabbed at her eyes. "I can't believe you did that."

"It's not a done deal, so don't start planning the wedding quite yet. I'll keep you posted."

She jumped up and took Jared by surprise with a big hug. "You are too much, Mr. James."

"It's no big deal."

"It's a very big deal." Alex extended his hand. "We appreciate it."

Jared shrugged off their praise but was acutely aware of Lizzie watching the exchange with interest. Maybe he shouldn't have told Alex and Jenny the news in front of her in light of their differing philosophies about money and all the perks that came with it. "I'll let you know when I hear back from the broker."

Jenny, Alex and Paul left a few minutes later, followed by Victoria and Shannon, which left him finally alone with Lizzie.

He sat on the lounge chair next to the one she occupied. Taken in by the glow of the firelight on her gorgeous face, he was silent for a long moment, until he couldn't wait any longer to ask her the one question that'd been burning in his mind all evening.

"What're you doing here, babe?"

CHAPTER 4

"I can't believe she showed up after all this time," Daisy said to David as they shared the sink in his bathroom to brush their teeth. "Tell me every detail of where you found her and what she said."

David spit out the toothpaste, dried his mouth and told the story again, making sure to include every detail as requested.

"So she thought he was fooling around with Jenny *and* me? At the *same* time?"

"Apparently."

Wearing one of his T-shirts over a tiny pair of panties he'd caught a glimpse of as she'd undressed, Daisy got into bed ahead of him and propped her head on her upturned hand. "That's kinky."

David cracked up laughing as he got into bed wearing only a pair of boxers. "From what I heard before I actually met him, Jared had a heck of a reputation as a man about town back in the day. No doubt she's heard that, too."

"So she thought he'd gone back to his old ways."

"Something like that."

"Imagine if you hadn't seen her," Daisy said as she curled up to him the way she did every night.

David lived for this time with her at the end of every long day.

"He might never have known she'd come."

"He said that, too. He realizes it was a close call."

"Did he say if he was happy to see her?"

"It seemed he might be reserving judgment on how he felt about it until he heard what she had to say."

"It's a good sign that she came, right?"

"It could be, or it could mean she's looking for some closure so they can both move on."

"I hope that's not why she's here," Daisy said with a sigh. "That would kill him."

Her soft curves pressed against his side and her hand caressing his belly had him thinking about his own love life rather than Jared's. He tightened his hold on her and scooted down to better align his lips with hers.

"I want to go spy on them."

The comment made him laugh. "You're not spying on them."

"Come on… He wouldn't care. He knows I'm invested."

"What about me and what I need?"

Her brows knitted adorably. "What do you need?"

"You. I need you. This, right here, is what gets me through the day. Knowing I have you all to myself at the end of it."

Her smile lit up her gorgeous face.

He loved to see her smile like that. For a while after her ex-boyfriend attacked her, he'd wondered if she'd ever smile again, and now her smiles were frequent and dazzling—and all for him. "I love you," he said as he captured her full, sexy lips in the kiss he'd been craving since he left her that morning to go to work.

Her arms curled around his neck as she teased him with gentle dabs of her tongue.

David worked his hands under the T-shirt and had it up and over her head in record time. Nothing felt as good as her soft skin pressed against his. *Oh God, except for that,* he thought, as her hand curled around his erection and stroked him. "Daisy," he said on a gasp.

"Mmm, I love you, too. So much."

Already on the edge after only a few gentle strokes of her hand, he rolled on top of her, gazing down at her blonde hair spread out on his pillow. "Isn't this better than spying?"

"This is better than anything."

He couldn't disagree with her there. Nothing in his life could compare to the sweet magic they created together. Bending his head, he rolled a firm nipple between his lips, tugging and sucking until she writhed beneath him, looking for more.

"*David…*"

"Hmm?" He turned his attention to her other breast and gave it equal time.

Her tight grip on his hair demanded his attention as he kissed his way down the front of her. Grasping her panties, he tugged them down her legs and over her feet.

She held out her arms to him, welcoming him into her sweet embrace.

He went willingly, powerless to resist her when she looked at him with such love and longing in her expressive eyes.

Daisy wrapped her arms and legs around him, took him into her body and arched her back. Her lips on his neck were like a trigger, sending a live current through him. Every time she touched him it was like the first time all over again.

He took her slowly, wanting to draw out the pleasure as long as he could.

She clung to him, her fingertips digging into his back, her legs tightening around his hips.

The tight grip of her internal muscles derailed his plans to go slowly. He picked up the pace, rocking into her over and over again as he captured her lips in another incendiary kiss. She did this to him every time. She made him forget everything except the incredible high of losing himself in her.

And the high was indeed incredible, especially when they reached it together like they did this time. He loved that she was no longer shy about letting him hear how much she loved the way he made her feel. Her cries of pleasure did him in, and he finally let himself join her, making some noise of his own.

One of the things he loved best about making love to Daisy was the way she always soothed him afterward with soft strokes of her hand on his back and her fingers sliding through his hair. He knew absolute contentment in the arms of the woman he loved and could only hope his friend Jared would find a way back to the woman he loved.

Now that the moment was upon her, Elisabeth couldn't think of a single thing to say. Watching Jared interact with his new friends had been illuminating. She'd seen their genuine affection for him and the generosity he'd shown in opening his home to them. Not to mention what he'd apparently done for Alex and Jenny. As incredible as it was, it was that kind of gesture that brought home how different they were. Those differences had caused her to often wonder if their relationship could work long term despite the incredible love they'd felt for each other almost from the very first night they spent together.

"Lizzie?" he said softly. "Are you going to tell me why you're here?"

"I wanted to see you. I've missed you."

He blew out a long deep breath filled with what sounded like angst. She couldn't be sure. She'd never seen him filled with angst. She'd known only the happy, cocky, overly confident Jared James. The Jared sitting on the lounge next to hers was so far removed from that guy, she almost didn't recognize him.

He was diminished, hesitant, wary and uncertain—four words she'd never have used to describe the Jared she knew and loved.

Even his hair was different. He'd let it grow out from the close-cropped cut he favored in the city. She'd never seen it so long but had to confess she liked it—a lot. Despite the other changes she saw in him, he was even hotter than he'd been before, if that was possible.

"I missed you, too."

He wasn't going to make this easy on her. Not that she could blame him after she'd ruined everything. She swallowed the hard lump that had formed in her throat and forced herself to continue. "I wanted to explain…"

"That's okay. You don't have to. It was really good of you to come here and all, but I don't need any explanations."

"*I* need it! I need you to know why."

"What does it matter, Elisabeth?"

That he called her by her full name hit her like a shot to the heart. He hadn't called her Elisabeth since the night they met when he'd decided she would be his Lizzie. He'd never called her anything else, except for honey, baby, babe and sweetheart. She'd teased him about how he refused to settle on any one endearment, preferring to make use of them all. "I'm too late," she said, trying to resign herself to a bleak future that didn't include Jared at the center of it.

As if he could no longer sit still, he got up suddenly to bank the fire. He squatted before the stone pit that was built into the pool deck, his shoulders rigid with tension as he tended to the fire with stabbing motions.

She couldn't stand to see him so wound up, especially knowing she had caused his dismay. Quietly, she moved to the end of the chair he'd occupied and rested her hands on his bare shoulders.

His sharp intake of air was audible over the cricket music coming from the nearby bushes.

"I'm so sorry, Jared," she whispered as tears rolled down her cheeks. "I didn't mean for this to happen."

"What did you think would happen when you turned me down?"

"I didn't mean to turn you down. I... You caught me off guard, and I wasn't prepared..."

Remaining in a squat, he turned to face her. "You didn't mean to turn me down? Then why'd you say no?"

"I didn't intend to. I shook my head because it was happening too fast, and I couldn't process it. But I never actually said no."

"Lizzie... Yes, you did."

"No, I didn't."

"So what you're saying is you didn't actually turn down my proposal?"

"I didn't turn down your proposal."

He tilted his head like he was trying to get a read on her, the gesture so familiar and so totally him that she couldn't stop herself from placing her hands on his face.

His eyes closed as he released another deep breath that shuddered through his big body. "Don't do this to me, Lizzie. I can't handle it. You broke me. You have no idea…"

"I think I do. You broke me when you wouldn't take my calls or respond to my texts. I couldn't sleep or eat. I couldn't find you. No one would tell me where you were. I didn't even know you owned a place out here."

"You couldn't eat?" he asked softly, his gaze filled with concern.

She knew he was asking whether she'd suffered a setback in her recovery and appreciated that he remembered and cared so much. "Because I was upset, not because of the anorexia. I swear."

"Thank goodness." He curled his hands around her wrists and pressed his lips into one of her palms.

Elisabeth felt the charge of that small connection throughout her entire body. "How did you find me?"

"I finally wore down Marcy, but you have to promise not to fire her."

"What do you mean 'finally'?"

"I've been to your office every day since that night."

"That's four trains. Each way."

"Believe me, I know. You won't fire Marcy, will you?"

"I won't fire Marcy."

"Good."

"Why did you shake your head when I asked you to marry me?"

"You caught me by surprise."

"How could you be surprised after everything we'd shared? You knew how much I loved you. I've never loved anyone the way I loved you. You *knew* that."

"Past tense?"

"I… I don't know. I just don't know. You've caught *me* by surprise this time."

"Does that make us even?"

His sinfully sexy lips curved into the slightest of smiles, which she took as a small victory. She'd made him smile. "I should get going."

"Going where?"

"Back to town to find a hotel, since I missed the last boat."

"You can stay here, Lizzie."

"I don't want to put you out."

"You're not putting me out. I have five empty bedrooms."

She took it as a good sign that he wasn't planning to send her away. She wouldn't have blamed him if he had. "When did you buy this place?"

"A couple of years ago, after I came here for a friend's bachelor party and fell in love with the island."

"You never brought me here."

"I hadn't brought you here *yet*. The place in the Hamptons is closer to the city."

"I like this one better."

"You haven't even seen the house yet."

"I already know I like it better."

"I do, too. I've become quite fond of it in the last month." He stood but kept a firm grip on her hand as he reached for the backpack she'd abandoned on the pool deck. "Let's get you settled."

Thankful for the familiar feel of his hand wrapped around hers, Elisabeth let him lead her inside, her eyes glued to the back of the board shorts that hugged his sexy rear. From the first minute she'd met him, she'd been struck by his incredible smile, those sharp blue eyes, his crackling intelligence and the cocky arrogance that was somehow charming on him. In addition to all those things, the fact that he was incredibly good-looking hadn't hurt anything.

She'd found out about the money a few days later—days in which she'd spent every minute with him while he literally swept her off her feet into love. That first weekend had been dizzying, and he'd kept her off-balance ever since. She, who'd prided herself on being a level-headed, modern, career-oriented woman, had fallen hard and fast for a sweet-talking billionaire with a heart of gold.

She'd become someone she'd always mocked—the woman who wanted to be with her boyfriend all the time, at the expense of other relationships, at the expense of sleep and time to herself and the extra hours she'd always given to the important work she did on behalf of homeless women and children. She wanted to be with him every second of every day.

He showed her to a bedroom that included an en suite bathroom. "Is this okay?"

Elisabeth didn't tell him she'd much rather share his bed like she had every night for a year. Instead, she nodded. "It's lovely. Thank you." She wasn't sure what she was supposed to do now. Should she release his hand and send him on his way? Or should she do what she really wanted and ask him to stay? Even if just for a little while longer.

"I'm glad you're here," he said after a brief silence.

"I'm glad to be here. Will you stay awhile?"

The battle he waged with himself was plainly obvious to her, but only because she knew him so well. "Sure."

It wasn't a resounding "sure," but she'd take it. She released his hand to remove her sandals. "I'll be out in a minute." Taking her backpack with her, she went into the bathroom to freshen up and change. She debated over her limited options—a tank top and boy shorts or the silk nightgown she'd brought in case things went really well. Fearing the nightgown would send the wrong message, she settled on the tank and shorts. He'd always told her he loved her in anything—and nothing. The memory of that nearly doubled her over in pain. The possibility that they'd never get back to where they'd been was almost too much to bear.

She brushed her teeth and hair and waited until she'd gotten herself together before she returned to the bedroom. He'd stretched out on top of the bed, and she took a moment to appreciate the well-defined pecs, the golden blond hair on his chest and the rippling muscles on his belly. She'd never understood how he managed to spend twelve hours a day at work and still stay so incredibly buff.

Suddenly, she felt self-conscious about the amount of skin she had on display and what her extreme thinness would say about how upset she'd been. When he took a greedy look at her, she wished she'd gone with the nightgown.

He held up the covers, inviting her into bed.

Anxious to be covered, she scooted under the white comforter with the yellow daisies. "I like this room. Did you do it yourself?"

"Hell no," he said with a scoffing laugh. "Sydney Donovan did the house. She's a decorator on the island."

"She did a nice job."

"Yes, she did."

"Are we going to talk about comforters and paint, Jared?"

"I don't know. Are we?"

"It's safer."

"Probably," he acknowledged. "I don't know what I'm supposed to do or say right now, and that never happens. I always know what to do and what to say."

Because she couldn't help it, because she'd missed him so terribly and because she loved him more than anything, she reached for him. "You could hold me. I've missed having your arms around me."

For a second she thought he might reject her, but he didn't. Rather, he slid under the covers and put his arms around her.

Elisabeth released a sigh full of relief as she pressed her face against his chest and heard the strong beat of his heart for the first time in far too long. Acting out of habit, she slid her leg between his and closed her eyes against the burn of tears at the familiar scratch of his hairy legs against her much smoother skin.

He held her so closely, so tightly she could barely breathe. "Lizzie... God, am I dreaming this? Are you really here with me?"

"I'm here. I'm right here."

And then he was kissing her and stealing the breath from her lungs with his fierce possession of her mouth. He quite simply devoured her. All she could do was surrender to him, which she did willingly. She met every stroke of his tongue with one of her own, wanting to give him everything he needed.

He pulled away abruptly, startling her. "What?"

"I can't do this. I can't be with you this way unless I know you're here to stay. Are you?"

She wanted to say an emphatic yes so he'd go back to kissing her, but she couldn't do that. Not yet anyway. "I... I don't know, Jared. We have so much we still need to talk about."

"Then we'll talk, but until we do, I can't do this. I'm not Superman, Lizzie. I'm not made of steel."

She blinked back tears brought on by the pain she saw etched into his face. "I'm so sorry I hurt you. I never meant for that to happen."

He leaned in to kiss her cheek. "Get some sleep. We'll talk more tomorrow."

Elisabeth watched him go, remembering how he'd once told her he couldn't stand to sleep without her on the rare nights they'd spent apart, all due to his business obligations. She could only hope they could find their way back to each other, because she hated sleeping without him, too.

CHAPTER 5

Knowing he was too keyed up—and turned on—to have any prayer of sleeping, Jared went outside to the pool, where he swam twenty-five laps in an effort to do something productive with the energy zinging through his veins. Lizzie had come back. She'd gone to his office every day, hoping Marcy would tell her where he was.

Why hadn't Marcy told him that? *Because, asshole, you told her you didn't want to hear from Lizzie, and she took you at your word.* God, was it true that she hadn't actually declined his proposal? Was it possible he'd read the whole thing so wrong and had subjected them both to more than five weeks of hell all because his ego was so huge he couldn't imagine that the woman he loved had actually rejected him?

Still, he hadn't imagined that she'd shaken her head after he proposed to her. That meant "no" in any language. He'd relived that moment over and over again, and the shock of it still had the power to reduce him to tears if he allowed himself to go there.

"Not going there," he said out loud as he floated on his back and stared up at the stars dotting the sky. That was one of the things he truly loved about Gansett. It was so dark that the stars seemed almost close enough to touch. He'd never been anywhere that allowed for better stargazing than the island that had come to feel like home in the last few weeks.

He'd made real friends here, the kind he used to have before he made a shit ton of money and found himself separated from the people he'd grown up with. Any time they contacted him now it was because they needed something only he and his money could provide. He'd stopped taking their calls once he realized they were all the same. Even his own siblings had become people he barely recognized after he struck it rich.

Lizzie had become the one person in his life he could count on to keep it real. She didn't give a shit about his money. She never asked him for anything. Rather, she was often visibly uncomfortable when he tried to do things for her or give her things that most women would love. His Lizzie wasn't most women. He'd known that right from the start. She'd called him out on his bullshit, cut him down to size with her sharp rejoinders and made him want to be a better man so he might be worthy of her.

He'd never been happier in his life than when he'd been with her. Until she shook her head at that pivotal moment and crushed him. Having her back in his arms, even for a few short minutes, had brought home the magnitude of what he'd become without her. He barely recognized the face in the mirror each morning. The once-confident king of Wall Street had been demolished by love. Imagine that.

He uttered a laugh that became a groan when he pictured her in the tank top and boy shorts that had starred in all his fantasies since he last saw her. She had no idea how incredibly beautiful she was to him, and the sight of her in the simple yet revealing outfit had made him want to beg her to take him back, to forgive him for any sins he might've committed.

He'd noticed, however, that she'd lost weight she didn't have to lose. He'd seen it in her face, where her cheekbones were more prominent, as well as the sharpness of her hip bones. The thought of her not eating because she was upset over what had happened between them made him sick with worry.

It pained him to realize he'd do anything, give up everything, to have her back in his arms. It pained him to know she was sleeping in his house, and he'd been stupid enough to think he could actually sleep knowing she was there, within reach yet still so far out of reach. Wearily, he pushed himself out of the pool and sat on the deck for a long time, thinking it through from every angle while wondering—and fearing—what tomorrow would bring.

Lizzie was awake early. She wasn't entirely certain she'd actually slept, and if the aches in her neck and eyes were any indication, the sleep she'd gotten hadn't been refreshing. There'd been weird dreams in which she'd run after Jared and he'd moved quickly out of reach. She hoped the dreams weren't a metaphor for how this day would unfold.

Dragging herself out of the comfortable bed, in which she'd clearly done a lot of tossing and turning, as the sheets were all over the place, she headed for the shower.

As she turned the water on, another memory came to mind. Jared had always told her he loved the way she looked first thing in the morning with her hair all over the place and her face red and puffy from sleep. She thought she looked awful, but he loved her that way.

She turned off the water, brushed her teeth and ventured out of her room to see if he was up yet. They'd spent much of their time together naked, but she'd never felt more exposed than she did this morning, walking through the house, wearing nothing but the tank and boy shorts.

The house was truly gorgeous. Jared's decorator had gone with a subtle nautical theme that Elisabeth loved. She admired people who could pull together a space so effortlessly when her own decorating efforts resembled thrift-store chic, although using the word "chic" might be giving herself too much credit.

This was the kind of understated class that surrounded Jared in all the spaces he occupied, including his New York City penthouse, his office and the beach house in the Hamptons. Why, she wondered, had he bought this place when he already had a house at the beach?

They'd learned early on to avoid the topic of his vast wealth because it brought home the many differences between them that nothing—neither love nor time nor commitment—could bridge. He simply existed in a world so far removed from hers that she could barely fathom the differences. So they'd focused on the things they had in common—enjoying live music, supporting causes that mattered to people in need, sampling hole-in-the-wall restaurants and taking long walks in their city. These were things regular people did together, and during those times she could almost delude herself into believing he was a regular person.

Then he'd show up in a Bentley, dressed in a ten-thousand-dollar tuxedo, to take her to a benefit for one of his favorite causes, and she'd be reminded he wasn't like her. He wasn't like anyone she knew or had ever known. Her friends had told her she was insane for being intimidated by the money.

Most of them, herself included, still had staggering student loans that would take a lifetime to pay off. To them, the idea of a wealthy, generous boyfriend was a dream come true.

But Elisabeth had never been wowed by money or material possessions. Her parents had raised her to believe that money could never buy happiness, that true happiness came through meaningful connections to other people, work that made a difference to those in need and a life committed to looking beyond herself. One of her dad's favorite sayings was to think globally but act locally.

Elisabeth had embraced that slogan through her work at the shelter, where she made a real difference for women who'd survived abusive relationships, who were recovering from addiction and facing other challenges most people couldn't begin to imagine.

Her life had been unfolding exactly as planned until that night at the Ritz when her gaze connected with Jared's startling blue eyes. In the forty days she'd spent without him, it had become clear that she could, perhaps, go forward without him if that was what it came to. But she would never again be the person she'd been before she knew him. Everything was different now. He'd changed her in ways that might only be apparent to her, but they were glaringly apparent nonetheless.

"You're up early."

The familiar sound of his rough early morning voice startled her out of her thoughts. As she turned to face him, she realized she'd been staring out the bay window that overlooked the ocean.

He looked as exhausted as she felt, she noted on a quick glance. Wearing only a pair of running shorts, he stood with his hands on his hips, his pose almost defensive.

Chilled, Elisabeth crossed her arms over her chest to hide the physical effect his presence had on her. "So are you."

He shrugged. "Couldn't sleep."

"I didn't sleep too much either."

Running his fingers through his hair, he seemed on edge, restless and maybe a bit nervous, which was wildly out of character for him. Jared James was never nervous. In fact, she'd often accused him of being confident to a fault. Naturally, he'd scoffed at that. "Coffee?"

"I never say no to coffee."

Was it her imagination, or did he seem relieved to have something to do? She followed him into the beautiful kitchen and took a seat on one of the stools at the center island. Watching him move around the kitchen reminded her of many other mornings with him. He was a morning person. She was not. He'd enjoyed tending to her moodiness—okay, grumpiness—with coffee and breakfast he cooked himself and served her in bed.

When he plunked a mug down in front of her, Elisabeth realized she'd once again been lost in memories of the sweetest time in her life. As always, the coffee was made to her liking with cream and a hint of sugar. "Thank you."

"Let's go out on the deck."

She picked up her mug and followed him through the sliding door. "This is amazing," she said of the cozy teak furniture and potted plants someone had obviously spent a lot of time putting together. "I meant to tell you that last night."

"Can't take the credit," he said as he stretched out on one of the chairs. "Sydney again, with some help from Alex."

Elisabeth perched on the chair next to his. "I'm stunned to hear you didn't do all this yourself."

"No, you're not."

The teasing exchange almost felt normal. Almost. The pain was ever present, casting a dark cloud over everything despite the crystal-clear sky above.

"Could I ask you something?" he said after another uncomfortably long silence. "Anything."

"Why, exactly, did you shake your head that night? You may not have said the word 'no,' but that's a no by anyone's standards."

Elisabeth gripped her mug tighter, which was necessary as her hands began to tremble. Here it was. The moment of truth. "It was the same thing, the one thing that's stood between us all along."

"The goddamned money," he said with a growl of frustration. "Do you know I've spent most of my time here thinking about how I might get rid of it—all of it?"

Knowing how hard he'd worked for everything he had, Elisabeth gasped with surprise at that revelation. "Jared—"

"I'd do it, you know." He sent her an adorably uncertain glance. "I'd give it all away if it meant I could have you."

She hung her head in dismay. "You shouldn't have to become someone totally different. You deserve better than that."

"I want to deserve *you*. That's all I've wanted since the first minute I saw you."

"You do deserve me. I'm the one who doesn't deserve you. I've made the money too important. Not in the way some people would, but in another way that isn't fair to you. I don't want you to give it all away. You worked too hard for what you have to do that."

"What does it mean if I can't have the one person I love more than any other? What does it *matter*, Lizzie?"

"You still love me that much? Even after what I did?"

"Yeah," he said, sounding sad. "I love you that much." He looked over at her, the sadness prevalent in his expression. "I had forty sleepless nights to think about what my life was going to be like without you. I didn't like the view. Not one bit."

"I didn't either. I hated being without you. I felt like I'd had my right arm amputated. Watching you walk away from me that night... It was devastating."

"I shouldn't have done that. I should've at least seen you home."

"Richard took me home," she said, referring to his driver.

"It should've been me. That's another thing that's tortured me ever since. Why would you want to marry a guy who'd walk away and leave you alone in the middle of the city?"

"I wasn't alone. You asked Richard to see me home, and he did."

"Which is just another example of the many privileges I enjoy—including the ability to walk away from the woman I love because I didn't get what I wanted from her, knowing someone else will see her home."

"That's not how it was, Jared."

"That's exactly how it was!"

Mustering all the courage she possessed, Elisabeth put her mug on a table and got up to move to his chair. She couldn't stand to be so close to him, to see him so upset and not be able to touch him.

"What're you doing?" he asked when she approached his chair.

"Move over."

He looked up at her for a long, breathless moment before he did as she'd asked, making room for her next to him.

When she was settled, she reached for his hand and linked their fingers. "I love you, too. I love you so much, enough to put aside all the worries and fears about the money and the ideals I'd be sacrificing to spend forever with you."

"They're *your* ideals, and they're important to you. You said I shouldn't have to give up what I am for you. Well, the same is true for you."

"What good are all our beliefs and possessions and ideals if they keep us from the one thing we want more than anything else?"

"What if we both made some changes and gave up a few of the things that've stood between us?"

"What kind of changes?" she asked warily.

"I'm not going back to the firm."

"What? Wait a minute…" His partnership at the brokerage firm was such a big part of who he was. She almost couldn't imagine him without the custom-made suits and Hermes briefcase.

"I've thought about a lot of things since I've been here, and that's one of them. I'm tired of working twelve and sixteen hours a day when I already have more money than I can spend in a lifetime. I'm exhausted. I didn't know how exhausted I was until I had a month away from the grind."

"What'll you do?" The idea of him actually retiring at thirty-eight was inconceivable. He was too dynamic and full of energy to step away completely.

"I don't know yet, but I've thought about relocating, too."

"To where?"

"Here."

Elisabeth stared at him, trying to decide if he was serious. He looked to be dead serious.

"Do you know that in the three years I've owned this house, I'd spent a grand total of ten days here before this latest visit? Look at this place. It's like a slice of paradise, and it was sitting here unused for all that time. What am I trying to prove and who am I trying to prove it to? There're other things I can do besides make money."

"Like what? And don't get me wrong. I think you have many hidden talents, but what do you see yourself doing in this new life you've envisioned?"

"Maybe overseeing a foundation that gives away some of the money in a productive way. Maybe helping other people to put their money to work for them. I don't know. Nothing is solid yet except for the part about leaving the firm. That's definite."

"Have you told your partners yet?"

"No."

"What do you think they'll say?"

"They'll be pissed. I'm the rainmaker."

This was said without an ounce of ego. It was the God's honest truth, and she knew it as much as his partners did.

"It's just not what I want anymore."

"Can I ask you something else?"

"Sure."

"If things hadn't happened the way they did with us, would you be saying that you wanted out of the firm?"

"I don't know," he said with a sigh. "What happened with you was a wake-up call, though. I can't deny that. People like to say money can't buy happiness, and I've always disagreed with that. I grew up with nothing, so having money made me pretty damned happy. Until I lost the one thing that money couldn't buy, and the rest of it stopped being so appealing."

"I hate that I caused that," she said with a sigh of her own.

"You didn't cause it. You helped me to see that changes were needed." He glanced at her almost shyly, which was adorable. "What do you think of my island so far?"

"It's beautiful. I really loved your friends, once I got over thinking you were fooling around with Daisy and Jenny," she added with a sheepish grin.

"It kills me that you thought I'd be interested in someone else."

"You do have a bit of a reputation for such things," she reminded him with a teasing grin. She'd never once suspected him of fooling around on her. They'd spent so much time together, there wasn't much left for anything—or anyone—else.

"Not since I met you."

"I'm sorry I thought that. It wasn't fair of me to show up uninvited and then jump to conclusions."

"I'm just glad David saw you and convinced you to come back."

"Are you? Really?"

"Of course I am. The idea that you could've been here and I'd never know it..." He shook his head and then glanced at her. "What would you think of relocating from the city to somewhere calmer and simpler?"

"You're serious."

"Very serious."

"What about my job?"

"You've given the shelter ten years of twelve- and fourteen-hour days. Aren't you exhausted, too?"

"Sometimes. But they need me, and I need the job. I have bills that won't just disappear because I decide to quit my job."

"I wish you'd let me pay off your loans."

"We're not having that conversation again."

"Why not? Why won't you let me make your life easier?"

"Because I didn't set out to have an 'easy' life. I wanted a fulfilling life."

He stood and reached for her hand. "I want to show you something."

Startled, she looked up at him. "Now?"

"Right now."

There, finally, was the Jared she recognized. She saw him in the spark of excitement that lit up his eyes as he waited for her to take his hand and let him lead the way. How could she resist him?

CHAPTER 6

Jared hoped he was doing the right thing and not making everything worse by showing Lizzie the Chesterfield Estate. During another long, sleepless night, he'd allowed his mind to wander, to picture the ideal life for himself. Lizzie had been right smack in the middle of it as his fantasy wife and the mother of his fantasy children.

Their fantasy life had transpired here on Gansett Island, where he'd found true friends and a sense of community he'd never experienced in the city. He'd found people who seemed to like him for who he was rather than what he had, and the desire to make a life here for himself—and maybe Lizzie, too—had filled him with a new sense of purpose. He'd had a brainstorm at three o'clock in the morning that he was now eager to share with her.

After a quick call to the broker he'd met the day before, they took showers, had cereal for breakfast and set out in the Porsche.

"Where're we going?" she asked as they left his driveway.

"You'll see. Soon enough. In the meantime, enjoy the scenery." Gansett was at her most beautiful this morning with bright sunshine, brilliant blue skies and a cool ocean breeze. Thank goodness Lizzie had missed the heat wave a few weeks back, which had made life miserable for everyone, even those like him who were fortunate to have air-conditioned homes.

"The scenery is quite something," she said as they drove along a coastal road where they could see the day's first ferry steaming toward the island. "What do you suppose it's like in the winter?"

"From what I hear, it's quiet and cozy and remote."

"And that appeals to you?"

"Greatly."

She had no reply to that statement, and he didn't attempt to defend it. She either wanted what he did, or she didn't. He couldn't force it on her, and he had no plans to try. His plan, such as it was, included showing her the Chesterfield Estate, sharing his idea with her and seeing what she thought of it. The rest would be up to her.

He'd come to the conclusion that he couldn't change everything about himself to suit someone else, even someone he loved as much as he loved Lizzie. He could only hope that she'd see what he did when she saw the Chesterfield place and that his idea would appeal to her. If it didn't, they'd have to talk about whether their individual visions for their lives had any hope of matching up into a life together.

That was the only way this could work. He very much wanted it to work with her, but he was no longer willing to sell his soul to the devil to make it happen. That last bit had also been part of the middle-of-the-night revelation.

They drove into the long driveway that led to the estate where Doro Chase waited in her sporty red car. She emerged wearing a bright smile when Jared pulled up behind her and cut the engine. Was it his imagination or did her smile fade when she saw the woman riding shotgun in his car?

"What is this place?" Lizzie asked.

"It's the Chesterfield Estate."

"Oh, the one you might be buying? It's amazing."

Encouraged by her first impression, he said, "Come see the rest."

Doro greeted him with a handshake and another for Lizzie when he introduced her to the broker. "I've spoken to Mrs. Chesterfield's executor, and your offer is under consideration by her heirs."

"That's good to know," Jared said. "I'd like to show Lizzie the house. Would that be all right?"

"Of course. I'll unlock it for you." When she had the door open, she turned to them. "Would you like a guided tour?"

"No, thank you," Jared said. "That won't be necessary."

"Take your time."

"Thanks." He ushered Lizzie into the black-and-white-tiled foyer with the crystal chandelier hanging over a table bearing bright yellow roses, sunflowers and other blooms he couldn't easily identify.

"This foyer is bigger than my whole apartment!" Lizzie said, taking it all in with an awestruck expression he found enchanting.

"I knew you'd say that." She'd said the same thing once about the living room in his New York penthouse.

"It's true! Show me the rest, Jared. I want to see it all."

Her enthusiasm filled him with hope, an emotion he hadn't experienced since the night it all went so wrong between them. He focused the tour on the downstairs rooms, which would be ideal for what he'd dreamt up at three a.m.

"It's incredible," she declared as they stepped onto the wide veranda that overlooked the ocean. "Are you going to move here if the sale goes through?"

"No," he said emphatically. "Hell no. I don't need all this."

Her brows knitted adorably. "Then why are you buying it?"

"Truthfully? It's kind of embarrassing, and it's one of those things you'll see as proof of my excessiveness."

"This I've got to hear."

"Initially, I made the offer because Jenny and Alex love this place, and they wanted to get married here. Because it's on the market, their request was denied. I figured if it was no longer on the market but rather owned by a friend, they could have the wedding they both deserve." He told her about Jenny's fiancé being killed during the 9/11 attacks and Alex's mother battling dementia. "They're so happy together, and after all they've both been through, I thought they should have the wedding they really wanted."

"So you spent millions of dollars to do that for them?" she asked softly.

"It was nothing to me and everything to them."

He waited for her to express disgust over the way he spent millions without a thought when she knew plenty of people who didn't know where their next meal was coming from. He'd also given as generously to her shelter as she would allow, but financial support only went so far with her constituency.

Jared was completely unprepared for Lizzie to launch herself into his arms. He was doubly unprepared for the passionate kiss she drew him into. And he was certainly unprepared for the way his heart beat triple time at the thrill of having her back where she belonged.

"That's the most incredible thing I've ever heard," she said, her lips less than an inch from his. "You are the most amazingly generous person I've ever met, and I've been a total and complete fool. Can you ever forgive me?"

"Lizzie," he said with a sigh, undone by her genuine regret. "I forgave you a long time ago. I know it's a lot to ask anyone to take on me and my lifestyle."

"It's not a lot to ask, and it was so wrong of me to let you think for one second that I don't want you."

"I know you want *me*. That was never the problem, was it?"

She rolled her bottom lip between her teeth as she pondered his question. "What do you plan to do with this place after you get Jenny and Alex married off?"

"That's where you come in."

"Me? What do you mean?"

"I was thinking you might want to put your college degree to work turning The Chesterfield into a world-class wedding venue."

She'd gone to college for event planning and had fallen into the position at the shelter when she'd been unable to land a job in her field. As her eyes lit up with what might've been excitement, he held his breath, waiting to hear what she had to say.

"You want *me* to take this on?"

"Only if it interests you."

Scowling, she poked him in the belly and made him laugh. "That's playing dirty. Who *wouldn't* be interested in a place like this?"

"I wanted you to see that there's something here for you if you should choose to join me in my new life."

"You want me to join you in your new life."

"Only if it's what you want, too."

Again, her lip disappeared between her teeth. "What's upstairs?"

"About fifteen bedrooms that could be leased out to wedding parties and a suite on the top floor that could be made into a honeymoon suite for the happy couples."

"Show me."

He took her upstairs and showed her every room, watching as she took it all in without saying another word.

"Could I see the gardens?"

"Of course."

They emerged into the bright sunshine to find that Alex had arrived while they were inside. He was happy to give them a tour of the gardens he tended to personally. "You've got to see this," he said as they followed him up a gravel walkway that led to the circular driveway. They took a detour under a willow tree that opened into a secret garden behind a wall of hedges.

Lizzie gasped and covered her mouth as she took in the incredible sight of thousands of blooms in every shape and color. "Oh, Alex... This is unbelievable!"

"I can't take the credit, unfortunately. This was Mrs. Chesterfield's pride and joy. She cared for it herself. I just maintain it."

Lizzie moved farther into the garden, touching and smelling and taking it all in while Jared stood with Alex and watched her from the opening in the hedges.

"How's it going?" Alex asked softly.

"I don't know yet. We're trying to figure it out."

"For what it's worth, I hope it works out for you guys. She seems really great."

"She is."

"Jenny's on cloud nine at the thought of getting married here. Thank you for that. I can't tell you what it means to both of us."

"I hope it works out."

"I'd better get back to business. Nice to see you again, Lizzie."

"You, too, Alex. Thanks for the special tour."

"Always a pleasure. This is my favorite place on the island."

"I can see why."

Alex left them to go back to work, and Jared wandered deeper into the secret garden to where Lizzie was bent over a pink rose bush, breathing in the scent of the flowers. She looked so fresh and pretty and young with her hair in a ponytail that left her neck exposed.

He wanted to kiss every inch of that graceful expanse of skin, but he held back the urge. There'd be time enough for that if and when they were able to work out the rest. "What're you thinking?"

"That this must've been how Eve felt in the Garden of Eden. Tempted."

"You aren't comparing me to a serpent, are you?"

Her ringing laughter brought a smile to his face. "Never."

Seeing her laugh made his heart feel lighter than it had in weeks. Not wanting to pressure her for answers she might not be ready to give, he reached out to her. "Let's go to lunch, and I'll show you some more of the island."

She slayed him with the tender look she gave him as she took his outstretched hand.

He took her to the Oar Bar, where she marveled over the thousands of brightly painted oars. Jared insisted she have a lobster roll and clam chowder to get the full New England experience. She loved them both, as well as the view of the bustling Salt Pond.

"That's the McCarthys' Marina over there," Jared said, pointing to the right side of the pond. "They're one of the more well-known families on the island. David was once engaged to their daughter." Jared went on to tell her the story of how David had recently saved the lives of his ex-fiancée and her newborn son.

"Wow. He must've been freaking out the whole time."

"He said he's never been so scared in his entire life—or more determined to do what he'd been trained to do."

"She must be very thankful. I can't imagine owing my life or my child's life to my ex."

Jared raised a brow. "Do you have an ex who's a doctor?"

"Wouldn't you like to know."

"Yes, I think I would."

She tossed her napkin at him, and while she'd dodged the question, watching the playfulness return between them only added to the hopeful feeling he'd been carrying around all day.

After lunch, he took her into town, where they checked out every one of the shops that lined the waterfront. The only thing she bought was a black bikini off one of the sale racks so she could swim in his pool. When she admired a bracelet made of silver scallop shells, he'd doubled back to get it for her while she continued on to a store full of crazy hats.

Back in the car, he reached for her hand and slid the bracelet onto her arm. When it was in place, he brought her hand to his lips and lingered there, breathing in the flowery scent of her lotion.

"Thank you," she whispered, looking at him with liquid brown eyes full of all the same love and longing he felt for her.

He could no longer resist the need to lean into her, to kiss her with weeks' worth of pent-up desire.

She returned the kiss with an equal amount of ardor, oblivious to their location parked along a well-traveled street.

"God, Lizzie…" He rested his forehead against hers and focused on drawing air to his oxygen-starved lungs. "I want you so badly. You can't possibly know how badly."

"I want you just as much, but we haven't resolved anything. And what you said last night—"

"I don't care. I just want you."

She studied him for a long moment, seeming to memorize every detail. "Let's go home."

In the year they'd spent together, Elisabeth had made love with Jared hundreds of times. Maybe even a thousand or more. She'd done things with him that she'd never done with anyone else. However, as she stood before the mirror in her bathroom, wearing the silk gown she'd brought with this possibility in mind, it felt like the very first time all over again.

At this point, she was stalling, letting the nerves take over when she knew she had nothing to be nervous about. This was Jared, and he loved her. No matter what differences they might've had or might continue to have, she'd never once doubted his love for her.

She emerged from the bathroom to find him sitting on her bed, wearing only the olive-green cargo shorts he'd had on earlier.

As she took in the view of his muscular chest, she licked her lips, aching for a taste of him.

He stood and held out his hand to her, a twitching muscle in his cheek the only indication she could see that he might be nervous or undone by what they were about to do. "Come with me," he said gruffly.

Elisabeth took his hand and followed him through the living room to a huge master suite surrounded by full-length glass walls that overlooked the water. Sheer white curtains billowed in the late afternoon breeze. A king-size bed covered by a beige duvet took up one side of the room and a comfortable-looking sitting area occupied the other half. The lamps were made of shells, and Elisabeth leaned in for a closer look at one of them. "This is lovely," she said sincerely. "Your friend Sydney has wonderful taste."

"I'm glad you like it. I told her to keep it simple because I know that's what you prefer."

"I thought you'd had it for three years."

"I have, but I didn't worry about decorating it until I had someone I wanted to bring here. Sydney spent all last winter on this project. I was planning to bring you here this summer."

"You thought of me when you were decorating it," she said softly.

"I think of you all the time."

She slid her hands up and over his chest until they landed on his shoulders.

His arms encircled her waist, drawing her into his embrace. "You look beautiful."

"So do you."

"I've got nothing on you."

"How many times have we had this fight?" she asked with a smile.

"Not nearly often enough for my liking. I think we need to have it at least a million more times before we declare a winner."

"At least." Before him, Elisabeth had never made love during the day. Her limited encounters had occurred in the dark, most of them with men who were out to please themselves first and foremost. Since she'd been with Jared, her horizons had been broadened in every possible way, but again, as he walked her backward toward the bed, everything between them was new again.

"What's wrong?" he asked, perceptive as always.

"For the first time in weeks, not a thing is wrong."

"Then why are you doing that thing you do with your lips when something is on your mind?"

"I'm nervous."

"No, Lizzie," he whispered, running his hands up and down her arms. "Don't be."

"I feel like my whole life is on the line, and I'm going to do something to mess it up again."

"The only thing you could do to mess it up is shake your head."

The comment was so unexpected that Elisabeth couldn't contain the bubbling laughter that escaped from her lips. "So we're laughing about that now?"

"I didn't mean that to be funny," he said, his lips quivering with amusement. "But I guess it is. As long as you don't do it."

"I'll never do that again. Ever."

"Don't be nervous. It's just me, and I love you. I'll always love you."

She didn't want to cry. She'd cried enough over the last few weeks that it was a wonder she had any tears left. But hearing him say he'd always love her broke what remained of her composure.

Jared kissed the tears off her cheeks. "Don't cry, honey. You know I can't handle it." He continued to kiss her face, her jaw and then down her neck, making her shiver. "There're so many better things we can do besides cry." His lips came down on hers and stayed there as he lowered them to the bed.

Elisabeth loved the heavy weight of him on top of her. He used to worry about crushing her because he was so much bigger than she was, but she'd always loved the feel of his muscular body pressing tight against hers. Now she ran her hands up and down his back as her tongue tangled with his and his hand cupped her breast, rubbing his thumb over her nipple.

The sensations crashed through her, one after the other, each happening before she could process the one before. Filled with need for him, she worked her fingers into the back of his shorts, drawing a gasp from him.

"I don't want to wait, Jared."

With his forehead propped against hers, he seemed to be gathering himself and fighting his own emotions. And then he was gone, but only to help her remove the nightgown that covered her. He'd taught her to be comfortable with him, to be free with her body and to never be self-conscious in front of him.

But that was then, and this was now. She felt exposed and on display as his gaze took a slow, perusing journey from the top of her head to the soles of her feet while he unbuttoned and unzipped his shorts. As it always had, the sight of his naked body made her feel greedy with desire. If his rigid erection was any indication, he felt the same way. He came onto the bed, one knee bent, his hands on her knees as he eased her legs apart.

Elisabeth recognized the heat in his eyes as he zeroed in on the heart of her, bending to press soft kisses to her inner thigh.

She squirmed under him, wanting to move him along, but she knew from experience that he wouldn't be rushed. As usual, he took his time until she was halfway out of her mind waiting for him to focus on the place that burned for him. Right when she thought she'd have to beg him, he finally gave her his tongue. *God, he is good at this.*

She'd spent an inordinate amount of time while they were apart reliving moments just like this one, when he used everything in his arsenal to shatter her defenses.

"God, baby," he whispered. "I've missed this. I've missed *you*."

Elisabeth fisted his hair, which she'd never been able to do before when his hair was so short, and arched into the strokes of his tongue. "Jared… *Please*. I need you."

"I'm here, honey. I'm right here." He pushed two fingers into her as he focused on her clit, sucking until she came with a scream, the pleasure electrifying her entire body.

He stayed with her through the orgasm that seemed to go on forever, withdrawing only when she flopped onto the mattress, boneless and depleted from the powerful release.

She'd barely begun to recover when he was above her, arranging her legs around his hips.

"Are we still good to go ungloved?" he asked hesitantly.

They'd waited a long time before deciding to be tested so they could abandon the condoms. "Yes." She was on long-term birth control and had been for a while.

"There's been no one else."

"I know," she said but was nonetheless happy to hear him confirm it.

Moving slowly, he entered her, his gaze pinned to hers, which kept her from looking away even when the emotions approached overload level. "Lizzie… Feels so good."

"Mmm." She raised her hips, looking for more.

"All the time we were apart, the only thing I could think about was how I'd bear to live the whole rest of my life without ever touching you again." His hand curled around her breast as his lips surrounded her nipple.

The combination of his words, the tight press of his cock pushing into her and the heat of his mouth on her nipple brought her right back to the precipice of release.

"Not yet, baby," he whispered gruffly. He'd taught her how to delay her release to ramp up the pleasure for both of them. Curling an arm around her left leg, he picked up the pace, making delayed pleasure an even greater challenge.

Elisabeth clenched her teeth against the need to give in to the release he was building with every thrust of his hips. She could tell he was close by the way his eyes drifted closed, his lips parted and his breathing deepened, all signs she'd come to recognize during their time together.

"Lizzie," he said, gasping, "I love you so much. I need you."

She wrapped her arms around him, holding on tight as he took them both to the edge and then pushed her over as he came with a growl against her ear that gave her goose bumps. "I love you, too."

CHAPTER 7

Still inside her, still throbbing with aftershocks, Jared raised his head and caught her gaze. She couldn't believe the myriad emotions she saw in his expressive eyes. Mostly she saw the love.

"Lizzie… Marry me. Live here with me. Run The Chesterfield or do something else. Whatever you want. I'd give you anything, if only—"

Blinking back tears, she kissed him, lingering over the unmistakable taste of him. "Yes. Yes. *Yes.*" She kissed him again. "Any other questions?"

He shook his head, and made her laugh through her tears.

"In this case, head shaking is allowed," she said.

"You're really going to marry me?"

"I'm really going to marry you."

"What about the money?"

"What about it?"

"I still have it. You still don't want it."

"If it means I get to have you, I'll learn to live with it."

"Will you let me pay off your student loans?"

"Absolutely not!"

"How about when you're my wife? I won't want your lousy debt weighing me down."

Elisabeth smiled at the teasing glint in his eyes. "Too bad. You get me, you get my lousy debt, and I'll pay it off myself. Eventually."

"Are you always going to be this stubborn?"

"Yep."

He released a deep, dramatic sigh. "I guess I'll learn to live with it."

His play on words made her smile.

"What about the shelter, babe? I wouldn't want you to think I don't realize how important your work is to you and the many people you help."

"I love that job and the people and knowing what I do makes a real difference."

"You don't have to leave the job if you don't want to, Lizzie. We can live in the city. I'm sure I'd find plenty to do there."

Elisabeth caressed his face as she realized the sacrifices he was willing to make so she'd be happy. "There's a young woman who started working there about six months ago."

"Aimee?" He also paid attention, which she'd appreciated long before she drove him away with the shake of her head.

"Yes, that's who I mean. She's terrific. I think she'd do an amazing job as the director—maybe even a more amazing job than I can do after so many years. It takes a toll after a while, you know? No matter how many people you help, there're always more. It's a never-ending parade of people in desperate need."

"You opened my eyes to things I never paid any attention to before I knew you. That's why I'd like to start a foundation, so you can continue to make a difference, no matter where we end up."

"I think," she said tentatively, "I'd like to end up here, with you and your new friends and your new business and this beautiful house. And I'd like to be part of your new foundation."

He stared down at her, seeming to drink her in with his eyes. "You're going to wake me up any second and tell me I've dreamed all this, right?"

She started to shake her head but stopped herself, which made him laugh. "No. You're not dreaming. I'm here, and I want what you want."

"Hold that thought." He got out of bed and walked across the room.

Elisabeth propped herself up on one hand to take full advantage of the view of his very fine ass flexing as he moved to the dresser. Then he turned around, and the view got even better. She licked her lips, filled with delight that she had the whole rest of her life to look at him any time she wanted to.

"What're you looking at?" he asked with a playful grin as he got back in bed.

"My very sexy fiancé."

His face went totally blank, leading her to wonder what he was thinking. "Hearing you call me that... I just... It's amazing and humbling. We never got to the ring portion of the program last time." He reached for her left hand and slid a square-cut diamond ring onto her finger and then kissed the back of her hand. "Most people would say I have everything any man could ever want—more money than I can spend in a lifetime, three beautiful homes, cars that make me happy when I get to drive them. I can go anywhere I want, do anything I want, and I never again have to worry about money. But know this, Elisabeth with an S... None of that means a goddamned thing to me if I don't have you. *You* are *everything*. The rest is just stuff."

Elisabeth's heart pounded erratically as his words registered. "The ring is beautiful." And it was... On either side of the stunning center stone were smaller diamonds in a platinum setting.

"I'm glad you like it. I showed restraint."

"Which I appreciate," she said with a smile. "The ring is gorgeous, but your words... They're the most beautiful words I've ever heard, and they mean more to me than anything else you could give me." She leaned over to kiss him, lingering when he responded with unexpected ardor. "And you're everything to me, too. I realized that when I watched you walk away from me that night, knowing I'd hurt you when that's the last thing I'd ever want to do. I hope you know that."

"I do now." He wrapped his arms around her and coaxed her into another kiss that made her head spin. "You know, it's possible what happened on that rooftop will turn out to be the best thing that could've happened."

"How's that?"

"It gave us both the time and perspective to understand what we really want."

"You already knew what you really wanted. I was the one who messed things up."

"It wasn't just you, Lizzie. I knew you were skittish about the money and the lifestyle, so dazzling you with the rooftop and the tuxedo and the Bentley and the out-of-the-blue proposal was the wrong approach. I can see that now. I should've seen it then. Less is always more with my girl."

"You didn't do anything wrong. Any woman would've been thrilled with such a romantic proposal."

"Any woman except the one who matters most to me. She's one of a kind, unlike any other."

Smiling at him, Elisabeth propped herself up on her hands and leaned over to pepper his chest with kisses and little nibbles that she knew drove him wild. Pleased by his deep breaths and quiet moans, she continued down, giving his abdomen the same attention, running her tongue over the cuts that outlined muscles that quivered in response.

She loved the way he responded to her, how he made her feel that anything and everything she did to him was exactly what he wanted. Because he was a guy, there was one thing he loved above all others, and it was the one thing Elisabeth had never done for anyone until she fell madly in love with him.

As she kissed her way down the front of him, she remembered the long-ago night when she'd asked him to show her how he liked it. The priceless expression on his face had been a memory she'd returned to over and over again during their weeks apart.

She wrapped her hand around the thick base of his cock and squeezed, drawing a gasp from him that became a moan when she took him into her mouth. He'd taught her how to take him into her throat, how to suck on the sensitive head and how to use her tongue to bring maximum pleasure. After weeks of wondering if she'd ever get to see him again, let alone touch him so intimately, she wanted to show him how much she loved him.

Judging by the moans of pleasure, the thrusts of his hips, the tight clench of his hands in her hair and the trembling in his legs, he loved what she was doing. The one thing she didn't love, however, was letting him finish in her mouth, which was why his efforts to remove her became more frantic as she redoubled her efforts, intending to go all the way this time.

She took him deep and swallowed as she added vigorous strokes of her hand, drawing a loud groan from him.

"Lizzie, *fuck… Christ*." His hands tightened in her hair. "Baby, stop… You don't have to… Oh my *God*."

She didn't stop. Rather she kept going until he exploded into her throat, thrusting and crying out from the powerful release she'd drawn from him. His reaction left her feeling victorious and thrilled with the way he gasped for air as she kissed her way back to his lips.

"You totally wiped me out, baby," he said between kisses.

"If I know you, you'll recover in no time."

He surprised her when he gripped her bottom, his fingers delving between her cheeks to find that pleasing him had also pleased her. His touch electrified her, and the discovery had him hardening between them as if he hadn't come just five minutes ago.

This, Elisabeth thought, was how they were together—insatiable, endlessly creative, happy to spend long hours alone together with nothing to do but find new ways to pleasure each other.

With his hands under her arms, he moved her up to better align their bodies for what he had in mind.

"How can you be ready to go again so soon?"

"It's you, baby. You turn me on just by breathing."

Once upon a time, back when she first knew him, she might've thought that was a line coming from a seasoned playboy who knew how to tell a woman exactly what she wanted to hear. But after a year with him, she knew better. He meant every word of what he said to her, and she'd gotten to the point—over time—where she believed him when he told her no other woman had ever touched him the way she did.

Elisabeth sat up, straddled his hips and eased him into her, gasping at the pressure against already sensitive tissue. She was always sore after they made love, but sore in a good way—the best possible way. Wincing from the pinch, she lowered herself down slowly.

"Easy, baby. I know you're sore." His fingers circled her clit as he sat up and drew her nipple into his mouth, both of which helped to hasten his entry.

"Been awhile," she said, wrapping her arms around him as she sank down farther.

"Feels so good." His lips vibrated against her neck, setting off another ripple of sensation she felt everywhere. "Nothing feels better than being inside you." He gripped her bottom and moved her slowly up and down, creating the best kind of friction.

If she could've spoken, she would've told him that nothing felt better than having him inside her. But he'd stolen the breath from her lungs and the words from her lips with the subtle movement of his hips, fingers and tongue. It had been this way between them from the very beginning, a connection that couldn't be denied no matter how hard she'd initially tried to fight it. And she'd tried. And he'd pursued, winning her over with his relentless belief that people from different worlds could exist in harmony if they drowned out the noise around them and focused on the things that worked perfectly between them.

So she'd done that. She'd kept her focus on him, on them, on all the ways they worked so well together rather than the few ways they didn't. But looming in the background, always, was the reality of how different their lives really were. Every so often, one of those glaring differences would make things difficult for them. They'd managed to get through it. Every time except for the night on the roof, when she could no longer deny their differences.

"Where'd you go, honey?" he asked, bringing her back to the present with his gruffly whispered words.

"I'm here. I'm right here." She ran her fingers through his hair. "I like your longer hair."

"I wondered if you would."

"I do. I love it."

"Then I'll leave it long just for you."

Pleased with that, Elisabeth rolled her hips and was rewarded again with the tight grip of his fingers on her bottom. "Not yet," she said, smiling at him.

He bit his bottom lip, which he did when he was fighting to hold off, and intensified his efforts to get her to where they both wanted to be. She was so primed from his earlier ministrations that it didn't take much to send her gasping into yet another orgasm. She'd once thought she was good for only one a day. That was another of the many myths Jared James had helped dispel for her.

He was right there with her, holding her close throughout the wild ride, until they sagged together, clinging to each other in the aftermath.

"Don't ever leave me again, Lizzie. I wouldn't survive it."

"I won't. I promise."

The phone call he'd been waiting for came at nine o'clock the next morning. They were still in bed, where they'd been since the afternoon before, emerging only to accept a takeout delivery that Jared had brought right back to bed. Because the call came to his personal cell phone, he reached for it on the bedside table.

"Jared James."

"Good morning. This is Doro Chase, the broker for the Chesterfield heirs."

Lizzie's hand moved from his chest to his belly, letting him know she was awake. If she ventured any lower, she'd find out how awake he was, too. "Yes, hello. I hope you've got good news for me."

"Indeed I do. The heirs have accepted your offer."

"Excellent. Since this will be a cash transaction, I'd like the closing to be scheduled within two weeks. I have urgent business that will require the estate be turned over to me two weeks from yesterday. I assume you can make that happen?"

Jared could almost hear her gulp. "I'll do everything I can."

"Very good. Let me know when the closing is scheduled."

"We'll need to travel to the mainland—"

"We'll do it here. I'm spending fourteen million dollars, Ms. Chase. Surely they can come to me."

"Of course. I'll let them know."

"If you could messenger a letter of agreement to me today, I'd appreciate it. I've got plans to make."

After she assured him she'd send over the letter, Jared thanked her and ended the call, returning his phone to the bedside table. He put his arm around Lizzie and held her close.

"What plans do you have to make?" she asked in the sleepy, sexy morning voice that had been one of the things he'd most missed about her while they were apart. Who was he kidding? He'd missed everything about her and was thankful to wake this morning with the promise of forever with her.

"Our wedding."

She propped herself up, pushing the mane of hair back from her face. "*Our* wedding? I thought you bought the place for Alex and Jenny to use."

"I did, and it's all theirs as soon as we say 'I do.'"

"And when is my wedding taking place?"

"Two weeks from today." He loved the way her eyes bugged out of her head.

"Are you out of your mind? You expect me to marry you in *two weeks?*"

"You're lucky I'm giving you that long. If it were up to me, we'd be on a plane to Vegas today. I figured you'd probably want your folks there and maybe a few friends."

"Two weeks."

"Some friends of Jenny's just had a two-*day* engagement and managed to pull off a beautiful wedding. I figure with two weeks, we've got all the time we need."

"I have to go back to work on Monday!"

"You're probably going to want to ask for some time off since you just found out you're getting married in two weeks."

"Jared, you're acting crazy."

"I'm crazy, insane, over-the-top, out of my mind in love with you, and now that I've got you back with me—where you belong, I might add—I want a second ring on that finger, and I want it two weeks from today." He kissed her and then tipped his head and kissed her again. "Okay?"

Probably because she could see how badly he wanted it, she said, "Okay."

"You can go back to work on Wednesday. I'll take you. We both have things to sort out in the city. And you, my love, have a very sexy wedding dress to buy."

"How sexy are we talking?" she asked with a coy smile that made his heart flutter.

"*Sinfully* sexy."

"I'll see what I can scare up."

"Babe, I want to have this fight now so we can get it out of the way."

Her lips pursed adorably. "What fight?"

"The one about how I'm paying for this whole thing." When she began to object, he pressed a finger to her lips. "I'm paying for it, Lizzie."

"You're not paying for my dress."

"I'm paying for all of it."

"No, you're not."

"Lizzie…"

"Jared." The look she gave him left no room for negotiation.

"Please? It would make me happy to buy you a sinfully sexy dress."

"And I love you for that, but I'll buy my own sinfully sexy dress, and I'll knock your socks off with it."

"I pay for the rest." He went with a statement over a question because he really didn't want to talk anymore. Not when he had the love of his life naked in his bed. There were so many better things they could do besides talk.

"You can pay for the rest. But the dress is mine."

"Fine."

"Fine."

"Can we have sex now?" he asked.

Her tentative glance told him she had something on her mind.

"What?"

"Why don't you say it the way you used to?"

"Say what?"

"What you just said. You never would've asked so politely before I messed things up between us."

"You didn't mess things up on your own, Lizzie, and I was always polite."

Her brow lifted in a haughty expression that made him laugh out loud.

"Okay, maybe not *always*, but I was most of the time. Wasn't I?"

"You were *real* with me, and I liked it. It took me awhile to get used to your brand of 'realness,' but once I did, I liked it." Her hand lay flat against his chest until she dragged it down to his belly, setting off a chain reaction that had him hard and ready in under a second. "I liked it a lot."

Realization dawned on him all at once, and he offered a wolfish smile. "So you wanna fuck?"

"There it is!" she said, laughing as she reached out to cup his cheek. "Don't be different with me."

"I didn't mean to be."

"Don't be careful with me either."

He turned his face into her palm and placed a kiss in the middle. "I'll always be careful with you. You've given me the greatest honor of my life by agreeing to marry me."

"That's very sweet of you to say, but I hope you know what I mean. I want you to be *you*, Jared. The way you were before, not some cautious version of yourself. It's not going to blow up in our faces again. We won't let that happen."

"I got ya, honey. So are we gonna fuck?"

Laughing, she said, "I don't know if I can. I'm so sore from yesterday's gymnastics."

"Oh, baby," he said, kissing his way down the front of her. "I can work around that."

EPILOGUE

Two weeks had never gone by faster, Elisabeth thought as she stood before a full-length mirror in one of the upstairs bedrooms at The Chesterfield to take a final, critical look at herself before the biggest moment of her life. The dress was, indeed, sinfully sexy, clinging to her breasts and fitting tightly to the rest of her. While it was definitely sexy, it was also simple. She'd rejected dress after dress for being "too much," until she found one that was just right. There was no train, no bows, no frills, and she loved it. She only hoped Jared wasn't hoping for something fancier.

That thought summarized all the last-minute nerves she'd experienced as the days flew by in a flurry of activity. True to his word, he'd left the firm over the strenuous objections of his partners, who would feel his loss painfully in their wallets. But Jared had stayed focused on the life they had planned for themselves and the partners had finally accepted his resignation.

Elisabeth had given a week's notice at the shelter and proposed that Aimee be promoted to take her place. The board of directors had agreed, and though they were sad to be losing Elisabeth, they were excited to move forward with Aimee in charge.

Jared had closed on the Chesterfield Estate yesterday and had been ready with all the things they'd ordered from the mainland—and paid a small fortune to have shipped to the island in time for theirs to be the first wedding at the new venue.

Because of the short timeframe, they'd skipped invitations and spread the word digitally like the modern couple they were. The thought gave Elisabeth a fit of the giggles. He was modern and hip. She was always trying to catch up and keep up. She had a feeling that wouldn't change after they were married, thus her worries about whether she'd be enough for him long term.

As she worked her way through last-minute nerves, she tried to remain oblivious to the photographer who snapped her every expression. This wasn't just any photographer. Oh no... Her fiancé, being the businessman he was, had given exclusive rights to photograph their wedding to one of the top bridal magazines in the world, knowing the images of them and their fantastic wedding venue would bring The Chesterfield more business than they could handle.

Elisabeth had agreed to it because she couldn't deny it was a brilliant marketing strategy, but with the stipulation that the photographers and magazine team remain in the background during the wedding. So far, they'd been terrific about respecting her boundaries.

A knock on the door preceded her sister and parents into the room. "Oh, wow," her sister, Melanie, said as she took in the full ensemble. Jared had insisted on bringing hair and makeup people to the island for the big day, so she could have all the pampering she would've gotten in the city. Because she wanted to look beautiful for him, she'd chosen not to fight that battle and couldn't deny his people had done a masterful job.

Her hair was down around her shoulders the way he liked it, in an array of soft curls that were held back from her face by a single clip in the back. Tiny blooms from the Chesterfield gardens had been artfully woven into the design, and her bridal bouquet was made of white hydrangeas that Alex had cut for her. As her maid of honor, Mel wore a periwinkle gown she'd chosen for herself and carried deep blue and purple hydrangeas.

"How are things downstairs?" Elisabeth asked her family.

"Everything looks lovely, honey," her mom said as she dabbed at tears. "I can't believe how quickly the two of you pulled this off."

"I can't take much of the credit," she said. "It was mostly Jared."

"He's a good man," her dad said gruffly. "He'll take very good care of my little girl."

"Yes, he will." That much she knew for certain, and with that realization went the rest of her nerves. Everything was going to be fine as long as she and Jared faced the challenges that lay ahead together.

"It's time," Mel said. "Are you ready?"

Life with Jared would be as far removed from the life she'd imagined for herself as it was possible to get, but she had no doubt it would be a grand adventure. "I'm ready."

She quite simply took his breath away. Watching Lizzie come to him on the arm of her father, Jared could only stare in amazement at the woman he got to spend the rest of his life with. It could never have been anyone else, he realized as she approached him, her smile dazzling and confident. And as requested, her dress was *sinfully* sexy. If she hadn't come back to him, if they hadn't put things back together, he never would've gotten married. That much he knew for sure now.

He'd asked David to stand up for him, in large part because of his friend's role in ensuring that Lizzie didn't get away. The other reason he'd asked David to be his best man was because the good doctor was the first, genuine friend Jared had made since he struck it rich and saw his entire life change almost overnight.

His parents and siblings sat in the front row, watching the proceedings, but he didn't feel as close to them as he did before money changed everything. One of his goals was to bridge that gap at some point, but not today. No, today was all about Lizzie and their new life together.

When she and her dad reached him, Jared shook her father's hand, extended his arm to Lizzie and turned to face Judge Frank McCarthy, who'd happily agreed to marry them at the spot they'd chosen overlooking the ocean.

Their guests included the huge band of friends Jenny had introduced them to at the impromptu shower-slash-bachelor party she and Alex had thrown for them the weekend before. Jared and Lizzie had immediately bonded with Jenny's crew of island friends, including the McCarthy brothers and their wives/girlfriends/fiancées; Mr. and Mrs. McCarthy; their daughter, Janey, and her husband, Joe; Jared's decorator friend, Sydney Donovan, and her husband, Luke Harris; the island's police chief, Blaine Taylor, and his wife, Tiffany; Dan Torrington and his fiancée, Kara Ballard; and Owen Lawry and his fiancée, Laura McCarthy. Jared and Lizzie had enjoyed them all so much, they'd invited them to join in the wedding festivities.

Lizzie had also insisted on inviting Ned Saunders, the cab driver who'd been so kind to her, and his fiancée, Francine. The posse of new friends was just another reason Jared couldn't wait to settle into their life on Gansett Island, which would happen after he finally took his wife to Paris.

She held his hand and smiled at him as they listened to Judge McCarthy talk about marriage and commitment and the importance of love and daily laughter before he led them through traditional vows and the exchange of rings. Then he pronounced them husband and wife, and Jared kissed her, and she kissed him back, and he could honestly say it was, without a doubt, the single best moment of his life.

The elated glow stayed with him through the party that followed—calling it a reception was far too tame for what transpired on the Chesterfield lawn that afternoon. Jared knew he'd never forget the way she'd smiled all day. He'd never forget the way she'd felt in his arms as they danced for the first time as husband and wife. And he'd never forget the way she'd gazed at him with so much love when he carried her up two flights of stairs to the honeymoon suite Sydney had put together for them in record time.

After he carried her over the threshold, he made no move to put her down. Rather he studied her gorgeous face, trying to commit every detail of how she looked right then to memory.

"Happy?" she asked him after a long silence.

"I've never been happier in my entire life."

"Neither have I."

"I'm going to make you happy every day, Lizzie. I promise."

"I promise the same thing."

Smiling, he waggled his brows suggestively. "Wanna fuck?"

She smiled at him but shook her head deliberately.

He froze.

Her hand caressed his face soothingly. "No, Jared. Tonight I want to make love."

Filled with relief to have all the questions answered and a lifetime to spend with her, he kissed her softly and sweetly. "That I can do, my love. *That* I can do."

Thanks so much for reading *Chance for Love!* Join the Chance for Love Reader Group *www.facebook.com/groups/chanceforlove,* to discuss Jared and Lizzie's story with other fans with spoilers allowed and encouraged. If you enjoyed the novella, please consider leaving a review at the retail site of your choice or on Goodreads to help other readers discover the Gansett Series.

Next up on Gansett Island is *Gansett After Dark,* which will feature Owen and Laura's wedding as well as more from some of your favorite past characters and an introduction to some new McCarthy cousins! *Gansett After Dark,* Book 11 in the Gansett Island Series, is available now

GANSETT AFTER DARK
CHAPTER 1

The creak of the rocking chair on the new wooden deck, the warm afternoon breeze off the ocean, the heat of the baby asleep on his chest and the bustle of the town he now called home soothed and calmed Owen Lawry. Along the newly painted white porch rail were flower boxes containing the pink, lavender and white impatiens Laura had nurtured all summer.

Every square inch of the Sand & Surf Hotel had been renovated in the last year, leaving the scents of sawdust and fresh paint behind. They'd been operating at full capacity since Memorial Day, and it was indeed thrilling to see the hotel open and once again full of happy visitors.

Almost a year ago, Owen had stood on this same deck and watched the last ferry depart on Columbus Day. It had felt symbolic then. With that ferry went his old life as a footloose and fancy-free troubadour, traveling from gig to gig, following the seasons and the work.

He'd stayed that day. He'd stayed because of Laura. He'd stayed because he could no longer imagine a day—hell, an *hour*—without her. And he'd never regretted it. Not for one second. Her son, Holden, the child they were raising together even though another man had fathered him, was now as much Owen's as he was Laura's. Earlier in the summer, they'd been surprised to learn they were expecting twins together. He who had never wanted the constraints of commitment or marriage or family was now as committed as any man could be, and he'd never been happier as their wedding date got closer with every passing day.

Just one thing stood between him and the future he wanted so desperately with Laura, Holden and the twins—his father's trial. The thought of seeing his father again for the first time in more than a decade made Owen feel sick and anxious and fearful, as if he were still a five-year-old who couldn't figure out what he'd done to stir his father's wrath.

In a few days, he and Laura, his mother and Laura's father, along with several friends who would be testifying, would depart Gansett on the ferry and travel to Virginia for the trial. Frank was coming to help out with Holden while they were in court. Owen didn't want Laura to come, but she insisted on being there for him. He hated the thought of her sitting in the courtroom listening to the nightmare that had been his life in vivid detail that would shock and horrify her.

But he would've done the same for her. He would've insisted on being there, even if she didn't want him to come.

The screen door opened, and Owen glanced over his shoulder as his mother came toward him.

"I was wondering where you guys had gotten off to," Sarah Lawry said as she sat in the rocker next to them. She tucked her chin-length blonde hair behind her ear. "Is he asleep?"

"Out cold."

"You could put him in his crib, you know," she said in a teasing tone.

"I much prefer this." Holden's wispy dark hair brushed against Owen's chin, so soft it felt like an angel's wings.

"I always did, too."

Owen looked over at her. "Are you going to talk to Charlie before we leave?"

"I'm having dinner with him tonight."

"Will you tell him where we're going and why?"

"I want to. I need to. I know I do. It's just… It's hard to talk about."

"He deserves to know, Mom. He's been an amazing friend to you for months now." Owen directed his gaze to the ferry coming toward the breakwater, bringing another group of tourists to the island. This time of year, the ferries came and went all day and well into the night. "Think of it this way. You'll be talking about it a lot in the next week or so. May as well get it all over with at once so you never have to talk about it again."

"You make good points, and I'm going to try tonight. That's the best I can do."

"I'll tell him if you want me to."

"That's very generous of you, but it needs to come from me. I owe him that much."

"I'm still trying to figure out a way to talk Laura out of coming with us."

"I don't think that's going to happen. She's quite determined."

"I know."

His mother reached over to put her hand on his arm. "She loves you, Owen. She wants to support you through this. You have to let her."

"I know that, too. What will you say when Charlie tells you he loves you and wants to support you through it?"

"That's different. We aren't engaged or having children together, and he doesn't love me. Not like Laura loves you."

"If that's what you think, you haven't been paying attention to the way he looks at you. Love is love, Mom. You need to be prepared for him to want to come."

Out of the corner of his eye, Owen saw his mother shudder at the thought of Charlie coming with them to Virginia.

"I talked to John today," he said of his brother who worked as a police officer in Tennessee. "He can't make it next week or to the wedding. They have two guys out on medical leave, so he can't get the time off. He said to tell you he's sorry."

"So… That leaves just us, huh?"

All of Owen's six siblings had called in the last week to tell him they couldn't make it to the trial for one reason or another. For most of them it had come down to a choice—go to the trial or come to Gansett for his wedding. Not surprisingly, most of them had chosen option B.

"It's all right. Between the two of us, we'll get the job done." The only thing that mattered at the end of the day was seeing his father put away for a long time for the abuse he'd inflicted on his wife and children for decades, culminating in the vicious beating that had brought Sarah to Gansett last fall to recover. She'd stayed ever since and had been instrumental in helping him and Laura run the Sand & Surf Hotel and care for Holden, too.

"I don't know what I'd ever do without you, Owen. You and I... We've traveled a long road together."

"I was just thinking how Laura and I never would've gotten through the last year without you here to help us."

The comment drew a smile from his mother. He'd never seen her so happy or so at peace and hated the thought of the trial disrupting the hard-won peace for either of them. "Despite everything that brought me here, this year has been one of the best of my life. With some time and perspective, I can't believe I ever lived the way I did for as long as I did."

"That's over now. One more hurdle to clear and you're free."

"Two hurdles. Still waiting on the divorce, too. Naturally, your father is stonewalling the entire process."

"Of course he is."

"I wish I could've been there when his lawyer informed him that he has to pay half his pension to me every month."

Owen grunted out a laugh. "You earned every dime of it and then some. Besides, he'll be getting his three hots and a cot from the Commonwealth of Virginia for the foreseeable future. He won't have much need for his pension."

"What if he's not convicted?" Sarah asked, her brows furrowing with worry.

"He will be. There's no way he's going to walk with all the evidence we have piled up against him. David, Blaine and Slim will all be there to testify about your condition and injuries when you got here last October. It's a slam dunk."

"Except none of them can testify to the fact that they saw your father beat me."

"That's where I come in. I'll testify that I saw him repeatedly beat you. We'll get him, Mom. Try not to worry."

"What I really worry about is what'll happen if we don't get him. He'll come after me, and we'll all be in danger."

"He won't come near you. No matter what happens in the trial, you'll still have a restraining order that keeps him far away from you."

"I hate the idea of seeing him again. I know you must feel the same way. It's been a long time."

"Not long enough, but I'll do whatever it takes to make sure he can never lay a hand on you or anyone else ever again." Despite his intense desire to keep his emotions out of the equation, his voice wavered on those last words.

"Owen..."

"I look at him, you know?" Gazing down at the baby he loved with everything he had, Owen ran his hand over Holden's back. "He trusts me implicitly. He trusts me enough to fall asleep in my arms because he already knows I'd never let anything happen to him. How does anyone violate that kind of trust and hurt a child who depends on them for everything? How does a man become that kind of monster?"

"I don't know," Sarah said with a weary sigh. "I'll never understand how that happens. And you'll never know how much I regret the way you grew up, the sacrifices you made for all of us."

"I have no regrets, because everything that happened led me to exactly where I belong—and it led you to where you belong, too."

Holden squirmed in his arms but didn't wake up.

"I'm going to walk him upstairs." Owen stood, balancing the baby carefully. "Talk to Charlie, Mom. Let him in. You won't be sorry you did."

"Even if he insists on coming with us?"

"Especially then."

She smiled up at him. "You're a son any mother would be proud to call her own."

"It's all thanks to you. We don't give the sperm donor any credit."

Sarah laughed the way he hoped she would. "No, we don't."

"Have a good time tonight. I'll see you later."

"See you."

Owen left his mother rocking on the front porch and stepped into the cool lobby, where one of the young women they'd hired to help during the summer managed the front desk. She smiled at him as he went by with Holden.

He went up the stairs to the third-floor apartment he shared with Laura and Holden. They were going to have to find a bigger place before the two new babies arrived early next year, but for now, their rooms at the hotel suited them. In truth, Owen would be sad to move out of the apartment where he'd fallen in love with Laura and lived so happily with her and Holden.

He used his key in the door and moved quietly inside the apartment, where Laura was enjoying an afternoon nap. She'd been so tired during her first trimester with the twins. As with Holden, she'd also suffered from horrible morning sickness that tended to go on for most of the day. That was another reason Owen wanted her to stay home when he went to Virginia.

Owen deposited Holden into his crib and pulled the lightweight blanket over him that his mother had crocheted. Sarah fussed over the baby like a proud grandmother. It didn't matter to her, any more than it mattered to Owen, that another man had fathered him. Holden was his, and he was Sarah's, too. There was nothing either of them wouldn't do for him.

Before he left the baby to sleep, Owen bent over the crib to kiss his soft head. Closing the door behind him, he went into the bedroom he shared with Laura, who was curled up on her side, her blonde hair spread out on the pillow. Moving slowly so he wouldn't disturb her, he stretched out next to her on the bed and tried to force himself to relax. However, relaxation of any kind would be all but impossible until they got through the trial that had been hanging over them for almost a year now.

He tried not to think about the worst-case scenario—that his father might actually be acquitted. But even if that unlikely outcome occurred, at least his mother had finally left him once and for all. Owen and his siblings had spent years pleading with her to leave, but she had always gone back—until this most recent blowup, after which she had finally ended the marriage for good. His father was now out of all their lives, or he would be before much longer.

Without opening her eyes, Laura reached out to him, her hand landing on his chest. "What's on your mind?"

"Nothing much. Just taking a break next to my favorite girl."

Her lips curved into a small smile. "I'm a ball of laughs lately. If I'm not puking, I'm sleeping."

Since she was awake, he reached for her and brought her into his embrace, her head resting on his chest. "I'll take you any way I can get you."

"Love truly is blind."

"I love you so much, Laura. You can't possibly know how much."

Her eyes opened and zeroed in on his face. "What's wrong?"

"You think something's wrong because I told you how much I love you?"

"It's more the way you said it, as if you're worried I don't know. So tell me what's wrong."

Owen knew it was probably pointless to try to talk her out of coming with them, but he felt he needed to try again anyway. "I wish you weren't coming to Virginia." He paused before he added, "That didn't come out the way I intended it to. You know I want you with me no matter where I am. It's just this time... The thought of you hearing all that..."

Laura raised herself up so she could see his face. "Are you afraid it might change how I feel about you if I hear the dirty details about your father?"

"Maybe."

"It won't." She kissed him and gazed down at him with love in her eyes. "Please don't ask me to let you go through this by yourself. You did it alone for thirty-four years. You're not alone anymore."

Her sweet words brought tears to his eyes. In his wildest imagination, he never could've dreamed of the life or the love he'd found with her. Trying to contain the flood of emotion that wanted out, he closed his eyes tightly. He didn't want to be this guy—the one who was laid low by childhood demons he should've conquered long ago.

Determined to power through it the way he always did, he settled her gently back on her pillow and sat up. "My mom's going out with Charlie tonight. Why don't we take dinner down to the beach and let Holden get dirty?"

Laura looked at him intently before she nodded in agreement. "Sure, that sounds like fun."

He leaned over to kiss her. "I'll go to the store and get something for dinner. Be right back." Owen left the apartment feeling like he'd dodged an emotional bullet. He knew she was only trying to help him, but her sweetness and desire to help made him feel raw and unable to face the firestorm that lay ahead of him. Somehow he had to find a way to talk her out of coming with them, and he only had a few days left in which to do it.

Get *Gansett After Dark* now. Order a signed copy from Marie's Store at *marieforce.com/store*.

OTHER TITLES BY MARIE FORCE

Other Contemporary Romances Available from Marie Force:

Romantic Suspense Novels Available from Marie Force:

The Fatal Series

One Night With You, *A Fatal Series Prequel Novella*

Book 1: Fatal Affair

Book 2: Fatal Justice

Book 3: Fatal Consequences

Book 3.5: Fatal Destiny, *the Wedding Novella*

Book 4: Fatal Flaw

Book 5: Fatal Deception

Book 6: Fatal Mistake

Book 7: Fatal Jeopardy

Book 8: Fatal Scandal

Book 9: Fatal Frenzy

Book 10: Fatal Identity

Single Title

The Wreck

ABOUT THE AUTHOR

Marie Force is the *New York Times* bestselling author of contemporary romance, including the Gansett Island Series, which has sold more than 2.2 million books, and the Fatal Series from Harlequin Books, which has sold more than 1 million books. In addition, she is the author of the Green Mountain Series from Berkley Publishing as well as the new erotic romance Quantum Series, written under the slightly modified name of M.S. Force.

Her goals in life are simple—to finish raising two happy, healthy, productive young adults, to keep writing books for as long as she possibly can and to never be on a flight that makes the news.

Join Marie's mailing list on her website at marieforce.com for news about new books and upcoming appearances in your area. Follow her on Facebook at www.Facebook.com/MarieForceAuthor, on Twitter @marieforce and on Instagram at www.instagram.com/marieforceauthor/. Contact Marie at marie@marieforce.com.

Made in the USA
San Bernardino, CA
05 September 2016